'Tis the Season for Matchmaking

A Lasting
Love Affair
Continues

P. O. Dixon

'Tis the Season for Matchmaking: A Lasting Love Affair Continues

Copyright © 2014 by P. O. Dixon

Images Used in Cover Art :
Winter Beauty Woman © Subbotina | Dreamstime.com
Wintry landscape III © Strahil Dimitrov | Dreamstime.com
Brass locket © Horiyan | Dreamstime.com

ISBN-13: 978-1503111578
ISBN-10: 1503111571

Acknowledgments

A thousand thanks to Miss Jane Austen for her timeless classic, *Pride and Prejudice*, which makes all this possible. What a joy it is imagining different paths to happily ever after for our beloved couple, Darcy and Elizabeth, and then sharing the stories with all of you.

Heartfelt gratitude to Betty and Ken for helping to make this story a pleasure to read.

Table of Contents

"May your Christmas abound in the gaieties
which that Season generally brings."

Jane Austen

Chapter 1

The Proper Path

Elizabeth Darcy pressed her letter to her bosom. Cherished memories of her time spent in Bosley last spring flooded her thoughts, for her presence in the idyllic town by way of an invitation from her formerly estranged aunt Lady Vanessa Barrett, her father's sister, had been the means of putting her in Mr. Fitzwilliam Darcy's path. During those months spent in Bosley, Elizabeth had formed several other intimate acquaintances as well: Miss Lucy Lancaster, whose most recent missive also weighed upon Elizabeth's mind, and Lord Avery Holland, the future Earl of Bosley.

Folding her letter, Elizabeth breathed a heavy sigh. A second perusal of the missive's contents had further confirmed her suspicion that, in the absence of some act of divine intervention, Lord Holland would forever be contented with simply admiring Lucy as the dearest of friends. *How can he spend as much time in company with her as he does and not see that which is so clearly observed by anyone who has ever been in love? Lucy adores him.*

Elizabeth drew her heavy shawl together, opened the doors leading to the balcony, and stepped outside. Lifting her head, she breathed in deeply as she savoured the sun's warmth basking across her face. Everything around her hinted that soon she would enjoy her first winter in Derbyshire. Nothing compared to the deep sense of anticipation it instilled in her mind, for along with winter came her favourite time of the year—Christmas.

Christmases of late have not seemed much like Christmas at all without my dear Jane to share them with me. She bit her lower lip and walked over to the balustrade. Her mind drifted away to a different place in time—her last Christmas at Longbourn with Jane. *As my remembrances are the last I shared with my beloved sister, I shall treasure them for as long as I live.*

Ah, but this year held the promise of Christmas being unlike any other she had known. This would be her first Christmas at Pemberley with her wonderfully adoring husband, Mr. Darcy. For the first time in years, Elizabeth truly looked forward to the gaieties of the festive season.

Fingering her gold locket that held a clipping of her husband's hair, Elizabeth's reverie halted. As she did every day, she read its inscription — *A lasting love affair*. Her darling husband had it specially inscribed by the Lambton engraver who inscribed the one Darcy himself owned. It too contained a lock of hair — the one she had allowed him to take that beautiful spring day in Bosley when Darcy and she raced ahead of their party in his curricle. After walking along an isolated path for some time, engaging in pleasing banter of his increasing regard for her, the two of them enjoyed a tender moment on a grassy knoll. There, he leaned close enough to kiss her but, instead, tenderly begged her permission for an equally affectionate liberty. As much as she had longed for their first kiss, the taking of her hair meant so much more to her. What a lasting impression had been formed in her heart when he folded it inside his crisp, white handkerchief and then pressed the fine cloth to his lips and placed it into his breast pocket with a promise of carrying it close to his heart as a means of having her with him wherever he went.

Hurried movement in the distance caught her eyes. A warm feeling washed over her. She would recognise the rider approaching the manor house from over a mile away. She exhaled a deep sigh of relief over her husband's safe return from a trip to

Matlock to visit his relatives. Eager to greet him, Elizabeth went back inside the house. After stealing a quick glance in her mirror and smoothing her dress, she headed out the door, along the grand hallway, and down the staircase.

A tall, striking gentleman, Darcy raced across the black and white marbled tiles and climbed the steps two at a time as though his desire to see his bride after being away from her for so long would not be repressed. Upon espying his eager ascension towards her, Elizabeth stopped and waited.

What a lovely vision for his weary eyes. He took his wife in his arms in a manner befitting a man violently in love. "My dearest, loveliest Elizabeth, how happy I am to see you."

"I am equally ecstatic to see you too, my love." Standing on her tiptoes, she brushed a light kiss upon his chin. "Did you have a pleasant trip?"

"Yes, I did. You will be happy to know that Lord Matlock has agreed to join us at Pemberley for Christmas."

"Come with me," said Elizabeth, leading him by the hand to her apartment. "You must tell me all about it. Did he put forth a strong argument against the scheme—proclaiming we were abandoning long-held Fitzwilliam family traditions and the like?"

"You know my uncle all too well, my love.

However, he compromised when I reminded him how important it was that you spend Christmas with your family as well. I told him that, should he not agree to spend Christmas here at Pemberley, then you and I would travel to Hertfordshire."

"Lord Matlock does know that my family will spend Christmas at Pemberley, does he not?"

Darcy chuckled. "He knows now."

"And that bit of information did not dissuade him?"

"In truth, his lordship voiced his objections to my tactics. He would only be appeased when I agreed that we would spend Christmas in Matlock next year."

"A great deal can happen between now and then," said Elizabeth, arching her brow.

"Quite true."

Her mind agreeably engaged by her husband's news, she said, "There is much to do in preparation for everyone's arrival." She meant to head below stairs to speak with Mrs. Reynolds, the housekeeper, but the touch of his hand upon her arm impeded her.

"Where are you off to in such a hurry, my love?"

"I have to speak with Mrs. Reynolds and advise

her of the new additions to our holiday party."

"Surely that can wait," said Darcy. He persuaded her to sit upon his lap, thus rendering the eagerness in his voice evident. The touch of his lips upon hers soon reminded her why she considered herself one of the luckiest and happiest women in all of England. *If only everyone I love could know such joy.*

Later, the hour of the day did not lend itself towards prevailing upon his wife's lady's maid. Thus Darcy took up the task of fastening the tiny buttons at the back of Elizabeth's silk gown.

Leaning forward, he spoke softly in his wife's ear. "You are rather quiet, my love."

"I have been thinking."

"Should I be worried?"

Elizabeth turned and tapped him lovingly upon his chest.

"If you do not turn around, I might be persuaded to resume our earlier endeavours."

"I am happy to hold you to that, except I absolutely must not tarry a moment longer."

"Am I to hear what you have been contemplating, my love?"

"I received a letter from Lucy today."

"Pray all is well; more essentially, that she is not pining away over Holland still."

"Indeed, she is as much in love with his lordship as ever. Still, he seems perfectly oblivious to her feelings."

"Elizabeth, even if Holland were fully aware of Lucy's feelings, you will recall she is promised to another."

"Promised to another indeed," said Elizabeth, her expression heightened. "That is her parents' greatest wish. Lucy, on the other hand, wants nothing to do with the arrangement. And why would she when it is Lord Holland who holds her heart?"

"Surely her parents have some say in the matter."

She tilted her head and studied his expression. Having gone against his own mother's favourite wish that he would marry his cousin, Miss Anne de Bourgh, Elizabeth wondered how her dear husband could espouse such an antiquated notion. She folded one arm over the other. "Do you truly mean that?"

"Indeed, and there are also Holland's own feelings on the matter."

She glanced over her shoulder and their eyes met. "He loves her too. He simply does not realise it."

P. O. DIXON

Darcy placed his hand on his forehead and squeezed his eyes tightly. "I do not like the sound of this."

Now that her husband had completed the task of buttoning her gown, she turned to face him. "Pray hear what I have to say, my love. As you know, my aunt Lady Barrett is traveling to Pemberley for Christmas. Why must she travel alone when Lord Holland and his mother, Lady Clarissa, might join her? They are my aunt's family after all. It is only natural that we should include them."

"So, you want to extend an invitation to the Hollands. Does that include the earl? You do know the family's history, do you not?"

Did she ever! In fact, she knew more than she cared to know. The earl was effectively estranged from his family. His son practically loathed the man. His being there would cast a chilling pall over the entire party. Elizabeth said, "I am well aware that the earl may not attend. Based upon what Lord Holland has told me, I pray he does not."

"That makes two of us," said Darcy, barely above a whisper. "I fail to see what the Hollands' being here has to do with your friend Lucy."

"Why, I shall extend an invitation to spend Christmas at Pemberley to Lucy as well."

His mouth fell open. "Do you plan to invite Lucy alone or all the Lancasters?"

"What are three more guests?"

"Actually, you have identified quite a few additional guests. You must know that both Colonel Fitzwilliam and the viscount, Lord Robert, will join us now that Lord and Lady Matlock are coming. Having invited the Fitzwilliams, we are now obliged to invite Lady Catherine and Anne."

"Lady Catherine?" Elizabeth blew a frustrated breath. "Surely after the vitriolic letter she wrote condemning our marriage she will not come."

Recalling her aunt Lady Barrett's hilarious account of the lengths Lady Catherine de Bourgh had gone through in her quest to prevent an alliance between Elizabeth and Darcy, Elizabeth could only imagine the spectacle that would likely ensue with both ladies under the same roof for weeks. *I am sure the fireworks will rival all those at Vauxhall.*

"I am not saying she will come, but what if she does?"

Elizabeth refused to allow such a disagreeable prospect as spending the holiday season with the woman, who proclaimed her the worst thing that ever happened to the proud Fitzwilliam family, to rob her of her joy. She said, "On the other hand, I should love to meet your cousin Anne. Georgiana has nothing but good things to say about her."

Darcy said, "It seems, my dear matchmaking wife, that you have this all sorted out."

"Who said anything about matchmaking?"

"What else would you call your plans for Holland and Lucy but matchmaking?"

"On the contrary," said Elizabeth. "I contend that Lord Holland simply needs the right impetus. What better example than seeing how much you — one of his closest friends — enjoy wedded bliss to set him on the proper path?"

Chapter 2

Matters Such as This

Lady Catherine de Bourgh sat in her chair, surrounded by her daughter Miss Anne de Bourgh, her parson Mr. William Collins, and his wife, Mrs. Charlotte Collins née Lucas. In all her haughty glory, she looked as if she were holding court.

The proud lady had spent the best part of the morning fuming over a letter she received from her nephew Darcy's wife. Therein was a half-hearted invitation to spend Christmas at Pemberley along with the rest of the Fitzwilliam family. Indeed, her ladyship always looked forward to returning to the family home at that time of year. Not for the first time, she begged the question of herself — *How dare that so-called Mrs. Darcy presume to usurp the long held family tradition of the Fitzwilliams spending Christmas in Matlock?*

Sooner or later, Lady Catherine was bound to meet the little upstart who had snatched her daughter's birthright. That her Anne and Darcy were to be married had always been the fondest wish of her ladyship and her sister, Lady Anne Darcy, was widely known to everyone of consequence in England. Oh, how she had taught herself to detest her nephew's bride. Not only had Elizabeth Bennet robbed her of her favourite wish, she had also robbed her nephew of his joy of horse-racing. Having turned over the management of his interests to his cousin Colonel Richard Fitzwilliam, it seemed Darcy had lost all passion for the sport.

"Mr. Collins, I understand your cousin has invited her family to spend Christmas at Pemberley this year. I am surprised you said nothing at all about any of this to me. When were you planning to consult my wishes on the matter?"

"Your ladyship, I beg your pardon, but as my cousin's plans have no impact on my situation, I did not think to say anything. Again, I beg your forgiveness for my being so remiss."

She reared her regal head. "Nothing to do with you, you say?" Fashioning her lips in a manner reflecting her disgust, she said, "Are you not considered her family as well? Do you mean to say she has not invited Mrs. Collins and you?" Her ladyship knew full well that such an invitation had not been extended, having received a detailed accounting of all those who would be in attendance from Mrs. Darcy. She meant to cause trouble. What better way than to remind her nephew of his low connections?

"That is precisely what I mean, your ladyship."

"How dare she slight *you* of all people? Your being the heir to her father's estate entitles you to as much esteem as she bestows upon her father himself. She no doubt means to put on airs and pretend she is more than she is. I can imagine that her connection to horrid Lady Barrett has made her forget what she is about." Lady Catherine turned to Mrs. Collins. "My Anne tells me that you and my nephew's wife were once rather fond of each other."

"Indeed, Mrs. Darcy and I have always been the dearest of friends."

"She is not much of a friend, if you ask me; else she surely would have included you among her guests." Lady Catherine returned her fiery gaze to her parson. "Mr. Collins, I insist you write to your cousin at once and let her know that you and Mrs. Collins will enjoy Christmas at Pemberley with the rest of your family."

Without hesitation, Collins hopped up from the

velvet settee. "Indeed, Lady Catherine, I shall attend your command with alacrity."

Days later, Elizabeth sat in her sitting room reading her many correspondences. Her spirits brightened considerably when her handsome husband strolled into the room. "There you are, my dear. I was hoping to see you."

Crossing the floor with long strides, upon reaching her side, he leaned down and kissed her atop her head and then lounged against her writing desk. "Oh?"

"Indeed, for, you see, I have news that I can hardly wait to share with you."

"Is this good news or bad news?"

"I shall leave that for you to decide. First, I received a letter from my Aunt and Uncle Gardiner expressing their apologies for their being unable to join us here at Pemberley at Christmas."

Darcy's warm countenance faded. "I am sorry to hear that. I was honoured to make their acquaintance. I was looking forward to welcoming them to our home."

"I too am disappointed, my love. We must be certain to invite them to stay here at Pemberley with us as our distinguished guests when they travel to the Lakes this summer."

He nodded. "Indeed. I do recall your aunt having mentioned her desire to return to the part of the country that had been her former residence and where she has acquaintances who still remain." Darcy leaned forward, and he and Elizabeth kissed. A moment later, he said, "I shall assume that is your bad news. What is the good news?"

Elizabeth retrieved one of the letters from her desk. "I received a letter from my cousin today — a Mr. Collins. You will recall having first met him when you visited Kent last spring and again prior to our wedding."

Darcy rolled his eyes. Then he took his wife by her hand, led her to the nearby sofa, and persuaded her to sit in his lap.

The letter in hand, she fell easily into his embrace. "What are you about?"

He swept her loosened hair aside and brushed soft kisses along her long, slender neckline. At length he said, "If I am to listen to your cousin's nonsense, I may as well seek some enjoyment during the process."

"Now, why would you suppose the contents of my cousin's letter to be nonsense?"

"I have met the man." Tucking a strand of her lovely dark hair behind her ear, he commenced nibbling her earlobe. "Now tell me what Collins has to say?"

Lovingly swatting her husband's now wandering hands aside, she commenced reading the letter to the following effect:

Dearest Cousin Elizabeth,

I am writing to you on the urging of my noble patroness, Lady Catherine de Bourgh, whose wisdom I regard as unparalleled among all mortal beings, to inform you of a grave oversight on your part. While her ladyship in all her superior understanding likens your oversight in extending a proper invitation to Mrs. Collins and me to join our family gathering at Pemberley to a most egregious act of pride and caprice, purely for the sake of familial harmony, I shall consult my own conscience in this one instance and consider that you are merely outside of your depth as the new mistress of Pemberley and wife of Mr. Darcy, whom you well know by now to be one of the most illustrious personages in this land.

Rather than suppose, dearest Cousin, that you have forgotten your own humble origins, which would indeed be one of the greatest of all sins, I shall consider the fact that I never received a formal invitation to Pemberley as merely an oversight on your part. As I am indeed a member of your family, my good Christian consciousness will not allow me to consider it as anything else. While ignorance in and of itself is not a proper excuse, I shall not conflate your lack of understanding with malice.

Here, Darcy almost gasped.

Because she enjoyed laughing at the ridiculousness of others, Elizabeth's amusement could not be repressed. "Wait. There is more. He goes on to say that he and Charlotte will be delighted to spend Christmas at Pemberley."

"How wonderful," Darcy said in a tone that hinted of anything but enthusiasm.

"I cannot say that I am disappointed that my dear friend Charlotte will be here as well. I adore her." How she would have wished her friend had not married that ridiculous Mr. Collins. Charlotte, however, was practical. She even suggested there was no reason she could not be just as happy with Mr. Collins as any other man. Indeed, the last time Elizabeth had seen Charlotte, she *seemed* happy enough. *Could it truly be that happiness in marriage is purely a matter of chance as Charlotte espoused?*

"Having met Mrs. Collins on several occasions, I can understand your sentiments. However, that ridiculous husband of hers has nothing to recommend himself. What is more, my aunt knows how poorly I suffer her parson's company. I contend this is her way of repaying me for spoiling her plans as regards my future. Well, I shall not let her win."

"I am delighted to hear you say that, especially in light of what else my cousin has to say." Elizabeth commenced reading.

17

I shall close by telling you how much I disapproved of your father's decision to receive my cousin Lydia and her new husband at Longbourn after the disgraceful manner in which they comported themselves before they were married. I do not need to remind you of what a poor example it served for you and my cousins Mary and Kitty on the proper behaviour for gently bred young women. I told him as much in a letter. My noble patroness has assured me that her excellent nephew – your husband – Mr. Darcy is honour bound to refuse receiving the couple in his home. As a rector, indeed, I must concur with his decision.

Elizabeth said, "Are you not pleased to have garnered my cousin's approbation?"

Darcy frowned. "I do not know that I like being of one mind with that ridiculous man on anything, even a matter such as this."

Chapter 3

A Likely Story

Days turned into weeks and by now the initial wave of guests had arrived and the household had fallen into a lively parade of activity as everyone got settled. Lady Vanessa Barrett had what she considered a delightful surprise for her niece. When the proper moment arrived, she ushered Elizabeth aside and shared it with her. Indeed, her ladyship's joy could hardly be contained as she regaled Elizabeth with an accounting of the arrangements she had made for all of the Bennet daughters to be together.

Elizabeth's astonishment was beyond expression. She stared, coloured, doubted, and was silent. When she finally did speak, she said, "You invited Lydia to join us here at Pemberley?"

"Indeed. Are you not delighted?"

Struggling to put forth an appearance of composure she did not feel, Elizabeth said, "Pray tell me you have arranged for my sister to travel alone. Tell me that you did not invite her husband as well."

Now it was Lady Vanessa whose countenance clouded. "The Wickhams are newlyweds, but even if they were not, it would never occur to me to invite one and not the other. Why would you even posit such a notion, my dear?"

"Mr. Darcy abhors Mr. Wickham. He is the last person in the world my husband would welcome into our home."

Taken aback, her ladyship said, "I had no idea your husband and Wickham were at odds, especially as Darcy was the one to accompany the newlyweds to Gretna Green as well as pay for Wickham's commission in Newcastle."

Elizabeth's eyes opened wide. "How did you become privy to any of this?"

"Lydia told me by way of one of her many letters. She also said that Wickham often boasts of Pemberley as being his home."

"It is a pity that Lydia has ingratiated herself upon you in this manner."

"What manner is that?"

"With half-truths and innuendos," cried Elizabeth with energy. "I am rather certain she knows enough of the history between those two to know that Wickham is no longer welcome at Pemberley." Having learned all the sordid details of Wickham's egregious, mercenary, and even spiteful deeds towards her husband's younger sister, Elizabeth was certain Mr. Darcy would not take kindly to her aunt's scheme.

Lady Vanessa raised her palm dismissively. "What is done is done. The Wickhams arrive tomorrow. We must all simply do our best to get along."

Elizabeth folded one arm over the other. "Nothing has been decided in that regard until my husband decides it."

"Do you not consider you may be getting yourself upset unnecessarily?"

Joining the ladies, Darcy placed his hand along the small of Elizabeth's back. He bowed ever so slightly. "Lady Barrett."

"Oh, here you are, Mr. Darcy. I had such happy news for my niece, but I am afraid she is not as pleased as I had hoped she would be."

"Pray what news is that?"

"It has to do with surprise guests I invited to join us here at Pemberley for Christmas."

In a voice of forced calmness, Darcy said, "You invited people to my home without first consulting either me or my wife?"

Elizabeth said, "Wait until you find out who she has invited."

"For heaven's sake, one would be led to believe I invited Lucifer himself judging by your tone. Do you not consider that you may be overreacting a bit? This is your own sister and brother after all."

"Wickham!"

"Yes—Wickham. As I told my niece, I could not possibly have known about the trouble between you and your sister's husband?"

"In light of Lydia's easy omission of the truth, I will allow you could have no way of knowing before, but you know now, and I expect you to smooth things over with my husband. With that said, I will not have the next weeks ruined because of any animosity between the two of you." Elizabeth placed her hand on her aunt's arm and moved closer to her side. Speaking solely for her aunt's hearing, she said, "I shall not willingly be put in the position of choosing sides, but should it come to that you can have no doubt of whose side I will choose."

Stepping away, she said, "Now if the two of you will give me leave, I shall deal with the consequences of this unfortunate circumstance with other members of this household."

When they were alone, Darcy gave Lady Barrett a sharp look. "Your precipitous actions do not surprise me, knowing as I do how much you like to have your own way, but to invite someone to my home without first consulting me or my wife is going too far."

"As I told my niece, it never would have occurred to me that you would be opposed to the Wickhams being here. But now that I have a chance to consider it, I do not know why I am surprised."

"What is that supposed to mean?"

"No doubt you are uncomfortable with the thought of your lofty acquaintances meeting *all* your new relations."

Darcy had seen this side of Lady Barrett before and he began to consider that they had not made as much progress in their relationship as he had hoped when she provided him with a letter of introduction to Mr. Bennet all those months ago. Prior to giving him the letter, she barely tolerated him. She certainly had not been in favour of his intentions towards her niece. Had her ladyship had her way, Elizabeth would be married to her nephew Lord Holland.

In a less tranquil tone, Darcy said, "You do not know anything about me. If you did, then you would know why I object to that scoundrel's being in my home."

"Must you and my niece insist upon speaking in riddles? What could he possibly have done to cause you to hate him so? As a member of this family, I ought to know."

"I do not owe you any sort of explanation, nor does my wife, so do not dare speak with her on this matter again. Should I indeed allow George Wickham to enter my home, I shall only do so for the sake of familial harmony."

She placed her hand on his and gave it a gentle squeeze. "That is all I ask of you other than that you will forgive me, for I only meant to help. You and I have not always abided each other, but I do respect you. I would never willingly do anything that would cause you undue grief. I hope you believe me."

"As Elizabeth said, you could not have known about my history with Wickham. However, now that you have some indication, I will expect you to abide by my dictates with no show of discord—for Elizabeth's sake."

Later that evening, after a long talk with Darcy about how to handle the situation of the Wickhams' pending arrival in Derbyshire, Elizabeth drew her sister Georgiana aside. "Dearest Georgiana, I am afraid I have grave news to impart. It has to do with my sister Lydia ... and her husband."

"Mr. Wickham?"

"Indeed. You see, your brother confided in me what happened between the two of you."

Georgiana's eyes fell to the floor. Her voice unsteady, she said, "You must think me terribly silly."

"No — on the contrary, for I too was persuaded of Mr. Wickham's goodness by virtue of the gentleman's charms. You were young and trusting. He took advantage of you, much the same as with my sister."

"Thank you for not judging me severely," said Georgiana. "What is the grave news you were about to convey?"

"It seems my aunt was most anxious to meet Lydia and her new husband, and not knowing the particulars of the gentleman's troubling history with the Darcys, she took it upon herself to invite the Wickhams to join us here at Pemberley for Christmas. I do not need to tell you how aggrieved your brother was upon learning what my aunt has done. He refuses to allow Wickham to set foot in Pemberley ever again. Knowing all the facts, I am obliged to agree with him, but my aunt, not knowing the entire story, believes my husband is being unreasonable."

Her manners always perfectly unassuming and gentle, Georgiana said, "I am dreadfully sorry to be the cause of such turmoil."

How Georgiana reminded Elizabeth of Jane with her fair skin, her angelic countenance and golden hair. She placed her hand on her sister's. "You must not blame yourself. Lady Barrett never should have taken it upon herself to invite the Wickhams without first consulting Mr. Darcy or me. I thought you ought to know, for although Wickham is not welcome, Lydia is subjected to no such restrictions. There is no guarantee what she might do or say when they arrive, and her husband is turned away."

"Turned away?"

"Indeed, and should Lydia make a fuss, she too will be turned away. Suitable arrangements are being made for Mr. Wickham to stay in Lambton. My sister may join her husband if she wishes."

"Oh, Elizabeth, I should hate to think all this is being done on my behalf. The truth is, I do not hate

Mr. Wickham nearly so much as my brother hates him. I suppose it will do no harm for them to stay here at Pemberley."

Hours later, after yet another trying conversation with Elizabeth about how to handle the hornet's nest Lady Barrett had flung in their faces, Darcy sat in his study having drinks with yet another uninvited guest. He could hardly view this surprise guest as unwelcomed, however, for it was his friend Charles Bingley.

"I do not mean to intrude on what is meant to be a family celebration, but my sister Caroline insisted that we redirect our trip and come to Pemberley. She said she was feeling ill and she insisted she needed time to recuperate before we ventured on to the north." Bingley took a sip of brandy before continuing. "Mr. and Mrs. Hurst and I tried to persuade her that our visit would be considered an impertinent freedom. You know as well as any how persistent my sister can be."

A likely story, Darcy considered. Miss Caroline Bingley worshipped Pemberley and for as long as he could recall, she made no attempt to hide her ardent desire to be its next mistress. Judging by the manner in which she fawned all over him when he greeted the Bingley party's arrival, Darcy considered that if Miss Bingley was indeed ill, she must have immediately revived her health once she saw Pemberley. However, as he had given his friend Bingley a standing invitation to visit his home whenever he wished, he saw no reason to belabour the point.

"Bingley, I assure you that you are always welcome in my home."

"Thank you for your hospitality, my friend. We shall be on our way as soon as can be, for we are expected to spend Christmas with our own family in Scarborough."

"You are welcome to stay as long as you wish," said Darcy. What were four more guests after all, besides a most fortuitous occasion that afforded him even less time to dwell on that wretched George Wickham's freely roaming the halls of Pemberley? Darcy was certain he would take Miss Bingley and her obsessive sycophancy over Wickham's vile propensities any day of the week.

He ran his finger along the brim of his glass while staring at the flames dancing about in the fireplace. *Pray my darling Elizabeth will feel the same.*

Chapter 4

Less Varied Society

Her nephew's holiday party of family and friends had scarcely got underway, and already Lady Catherine was abhorred over the prospect of what the next weeks would entail. Her shortened visit to Longbourn had given her an idea of what she might expect upon meeting all the Bennet family. None of them had anything much to recommend themselves to her ladyship, and that included Darcy's wife, whom Lady Catherine regarded as quite unremarkable. *And this is the woman who usurped my daughter's rightful place as the next mistress of Pemberley.*

Her ladyship, however, silently rejoiced about Mr. Bingley's being there, for she much preferred the Bennet daughters chase after *that* young man than one of her nephews. It was unfortunate enough that the eldest had trapped her nephew Darcy with her feminine arts and allurements. As for the viscounts, Lord Robert and Lord Holland, her ladyship, shortly upon her arrival, began to consider that Anne would make a fine countess, and she commenced wondering why she had not thought of an alliance for her Anne with either of them before. There was the disadvantage that an alliance between Anne and the future Earl of Bosley must certainly be the means of always placing Lady Catherine in Lady Vanessa Barrett's company, but that was no reason to shun the possibility out of hand.

Lady Catherine was not pleased when she espied Lady Barrett headed her way. They had not parted on the best of terms when they last saw each other in Bosley; the former felt certain the latter had but one purpose in seeking her out—that being to gloat.

"I must say that you are looking far better now than the last time I had the privilege of seeing you."

Lady Catherine donned a regal manner. "Only someone woefully lacking in good breeding would dare bring up such an ill-fated confluence of events that resulted in my traveling back and forth between Bosley and Hertfordshire with the purpose of preventing a disadvantageous alliance between my nephew and your niece."

"All for naught, as it turned out."

"Had I not been betrayed by my own body, I dare say that I would have succeeded."

"We shall never know," said Lady Barrett.

As both young ladies were eager to spend time outside of Lady Catherine de Bourgh's company, Elizabeth and her intimate friend, Charlotte, stole away from the gathering for a private tête-à-tête in the music room. They had not seen each other since before Elizabeth's wedding when the Collinses suddenly removed themselves from Hunsford after Lady Catherine had been rendered so exceedingly angry by the contents of Darcy's letter announcing his intention to marry Elizabeth. Charlotte, who really rejoiced in the match, was anxious to get away till the storm was blown over.

Charlotte placed her hand on Elizabeth's. "Dearest Eliza, being with you like this reminds me so much of old times."

Her eyes lowered, Elizabeth half smiled. "Almost…"

"No doubt you are thinking of your beloved Jane and wishing she too were here. I miss her as well."

"Indeed. I often imagine what it would be like to have her with me still," Elizabeth said. "Oh Charlotte, pray you will not think me silly, but I have to confide in you that whenever I see Mr. Bingley, I cannot help but think of how perfect Jane would have found him had she ever had an opportunity to make his acquaintance."

Charlotte nodded. "Now that I think of it, I can see exactly why you would feel as you do. Bingley is perfectly charming and amiable, and — dare I add? — he is handsome and exceedingly rich."

"And neither of the two latter ascribed attributes would have meant a fig to my Jane in the absence of the former two agreeable traits."

"Indeed. But how do you suppose our Jane would have looked upon his pernicious sisters?"

"To Jane's credit, the entire world was good in her eyes. She would have found Mrs. Louisa Hurst and Miss Caroline Bingley to be charming creatures as well."

"No doubt — with *creatures* being the operative word."

"To you and me, to be sure, but never to Jane," said Elizabeth, her voice trailing off at the end.

"Indeed, never to Jane," said Charlotte, leaning forward to embrace her dear friend.

The sound of a soft voice drew the two women apart. Elizabeth wiped the tears welling in her eyes.

"Lucy, have you had a chance to meet my dear friend, Mrs. Charlotte Collins?"

Gregarious as ever, Lucy smiled warmly. "So, you are the lovely Mrs. Collins whom I have heard so much about."

"Indeed. I am happy to make your acquaintance, Miss Lancaster. Please, you must call me Charlotte."

"And you must call me Lucy. I am so sorry that we did not have a chance to meet at the wedding."

"Indeed. However, I am certain we shall have ample time to become fully acquainted during this visit." Charlotte stood. "If the two of you will excuse me, I shall leave you to talk."

When Lucy and Elizabeth were alone, they immediately fell into familiar conversation, speaking of many things: the easy trip from Bosley to Derbyshire, the number of guests, the plans for that evening's entertainment, and finally, the one topic which was at the forefront of both young ladies' minds—Lord Andrew Holland.

Lucy said, "That was a clever thing you did in inviting our family to Pemberley along with your aunt and the Hollands, not that I am complaining about spending time here in your beautiful home. Pemberley is magnificent."

"At first I did not think your father would accept, for our only connection is my friendship with you."

"Yes, but he was particularly impressed with Mr. Darcy's horse-racing acumen. Besides that, your husband is a gentleman of considerable consequence. My father was not inclined to deny such a man anything he deigned to request."

"I am so happy you could be here ... and Lord Holland as well."

"Again, I am not complaining, but I must confess that I knew what you were about as soon as I learned the Hollands were invited."

"After all you did in putting me in Fitzwilliam's path when we were together in town, how could I not do the same for you and Lord Holland?"

"But that is the thing. Andrew and I are constantly thrown in each other's path when we are in Bosley. It is a consequence of our rather less varied society. He simply does not see me in the way a man sees a woman with whom he wishes to spend his life. I see no reason to suppose that our being here at Pemberley will make a difference."

"I contend that once he sees how happy Fitz-william and I are, he will want the same for himself."

"I see, and you plan to concoct a magical po-tion and have Andrew drink it that he might declare his ardent love to the first woman he sees — who will happen to be me. How ingenious of you, my dear friend."

"I shall not resort to such stratagems, for I am convinced that Lord Holland is more than half in love with you already. He simply needs to stop fighting it."

Chapter 5

In Want of Wives

Mrs. Bennet said, "Mr. Bennet, I do hope that you have taken the liberty to put forth strong hints to Lord Andrew Holland and Lord Robert Fitzwilliam that you have two single daughters – whose connections are not inconsequential what with our Lizzy's marriage to Mr. Darcy as well as your sister's patronage – who are available as future countesses. Everyone knows single gentlemen in possession of good fortunes are in want of wives."

Mr. Bennet peeped over his paper. "I do not know that to be true at all, my dear Mrs. Bennet.

Wherever did you hear such a fanciful notion?"

"Why, everyone who knows anything at all about such matters as this knows it to be true, Mr. Bennet. Must you be so tiresome? Oh, how you do enjoy vexing my nerves!"

"On the contrary, my dear, I believe I live to appease your nerves."

"Then if that is indeed the case, I should expect you to do everything in your power to present our girls before the viscounts in the best light possible."

Mary said, "Mama, I do wish you would not try so hard, for I believe strongly that a proper young lady should not be in such a hurry. In time, the right man will come along and probably when one least expects it."

"You speak nonsense, my child," Mrs. Bennet admonished her. "Why, had I practised the sentiments you so self-righteously avow, I might never have married my Mr. Bennet at such a tender age as I did."

Mr. Bennet peered at his wife. "It is indeed gratifying to be reminded of how willingly I succumbed to your arts and allurements, my dear."

Giving her husband little mind, she prattled on. "You and your sister Kitty could learn a thing or two from your sister Lydia — married already and to a fine young man and she is but sixteen."

Mary pushed her glasses up. "I do not much like my sister's manner of finding a husband. I should like to think Kitty feels the same."

Elizabeth said, "Thank you, Mary. Those are my sentiments entirely."

Kitty shook her head. "I do not know that I agree with either of you. Mr. Wickham is the most handsome and the most charming man in the world—every woman should be so fortunate to marry such a man."

Georgiana, who sat next to Kitty, shifted uncomfortably in her seat, giving Elizabeth to know that a change in conversation was long overdue. Had Kitty known what pain she had given the young lady with whom she was forming a steady friendship, she undoubtedly would have refrained from speaking so adoringly of her new brother. However, she did not know; hence, she kept speaking. "Pray, Papa, you will allow me to visit Lydia and her husband this spring."

This being a sore point for the elderly patriarch, Mr. Bennet sharpened his voice. "I will do no such thing as you are well aware. I would sooner send you off to Bedlam."

Kitty pouted and Mary sighed and Elizabeth prayed that would be the end of that.

That afternoon, Darcy, Lord Matlock, Lord Andrew, Lord Robert, Bingley and the colonel were gathered in one part of Darcy's billiards room. The rest of the gentlemen, who included Mr. Hurst, Mr. Collins, Mr. Lancaster, Mr. Bennet, and last and certainly least in Darcy's mind, Mr. Wickham, were gathered in another.

Simply being in the same room with the man drove Darcy to distraction. Try as he might to put from his mind the image of Elizabeth's youngest sister in her tattered state of dishabille cohabiting in squalor in London's foulest neighbourhood with George Wickham, he could not forget what he had seen. How could Lydia be of the same flesh and blood as his dearest Elizabeth? To think she would be the aunt of his own flesh and blood and that vile George Wickham—his children's uncle. How on Earth would he endure his children calling *her* aunt and *him* uncle?

Darcy closed his eyes tightly to block out the unpleasant memories of recovering Lydia from the deplorable conditions in which he had found her earlier that year. He had done it all for one pur-pose—for Elizabeth's peace of mind. The pain she suffered upon learning what Lydia had done was so poignant. He wished never to see her suffer in that way again, especially after she had come so far in recovering from the loss of her eldest sister, Jane. Had he not found Lydia and Wickham and forced his former friend to marry the wild child, she would have been as good as dead to Elizabeth too.

He'd hoped he had seen the last of both of them when he parted company with them in Gretna Green, but he knew even then he was asking too much. He knew one day Wickham would come slithering around—he simply never imagined it would be as soon as this. His first Christmas with Elizabeth was to be tarnished by the likes of George Wickham. How was such a thing to be borne?

Darcy glared at the man who might have been the means of ruining his sister's life. *That despicable man.* There he sat across the room, imbibing Darcy's best liquor, toadying up with Mr. Bennet, who appeared to have forgiven the wretch for ruining his youngest daughter. *Whoever said that crime does not pay? Surely that old adage does not apply to Wickham.*

Lord Matlock interrupted Darcy's tortured reverie. "Darcy, I say it is time Georgiana has her first Season. Now that you have chosen your bride, it is time for your sister to find a husband."

His voice measured, Darcy said, "Georgiana is not yet seventeen. There is no hurry."

"What is the point in putting off your sister's coming out? As I was telling Lord Robert—"

Interrupting his father, Lord Robert said, "I am afraid this is Father's none too subtle attempt to advocate an alliance between Georgiana and me."

"Both of you could do a great deal worse than marrying each other. What say you, Darcy?"

"With all due respect, my lords, I say I would rather my sister marry someone closer to her in—"

"—in age?" Lord Robert said, effectively completing his younger cousin's sentence. "There you have your answer, Father. I am too old for Georgiana. Darcy said it himself."

Darcy shifted uncomfortably. "I was about to say closer to her in temperament, but now that you have mentioned age, there is that."

Lord Robert looked at Richard, his younger brother by two years. "I suppose that rules you out as a prospective husband for our fair cousin as well."

Darcy said, "Were I to object to Richard's marrying my sister, it would have nothing to do with his age but rather his want of a fortune ... unless they planned to live here at Pemberley. It would require more than Georgiana's dowry of thirty thousand pounds to afford her the manner of living to which she is accustomed."

The colonel said, "Let us not forget that I have always likened Georgiana to a sister as well. Then, too, there is the fact that I am one of Georgiana's guardians, which makes me much like a father to her."

Somewhat resigned, Lord Matlock huffed. "Darcy's having effectively ruled out his own cousins, one for his age and the other for his lack of fortune, leaves you two for consideration, Lord Holland and Bingley."

Holland, a tall, handsome gentleman, blessed with long, dark hair and amazing dark eyes, cleared his throat. "By the time I ascend to the earldom, I will be lucky if there is any wealth to speak of. It seems I too am to marry a woman whose dowry is at least fifty thousand pounds." Holland looked to Bingley and then to Darcy. "Besides, if wealth and youth are indeed what you seek for your sister, then you need look no further than Bingley here."

Bingley, who had been slouching, stood straight and tall. "If we are in the business of rounding up husbands, need I remind all of you that I too have an unmarried sister?" That was enough to change the course of the conversation.

Later, when Darcy and Bingley were alone, Bingley endeavoured to make amends for what had happened earlier.

"Darcy," he said, his voice filled with reticence, "I am indeed flattered that your uncle would even consider me a likely candidate for an alliance with your sister, but I believe I have already met the future Mrs. Bingley."

Darcy mentally calculated the number of times he had heard that last part of his friend's speech before. "An angel, no doubt," said Darcy knowingly. "I ought to be the one apologizing to you, my friend, for my family's presumptions."

Bingley gushed. "Darcy, it is a point of honour to be considered. However, I think your sister barely tolerates me — as much as it would please my sisters to suppose otherwise."

Thinking it better to put an end to their discourse, Darcy suggested they had better join the others. Walking beside Bingley, he considered how much he would be honoured to have his friend as his brother as well, for his young friend was blessed with everything a loving brother most desired for his sister. He could think of but one drawback — that being a lifelong connection to Caroline Bingley, whom he never really cared for from the start and whom he cared for even less after the manner in which she went about trying to poison his mind against Elizabeth when they were all together in Bosley.

What great pride Miss Bingley had taken in confiding in him how objectionable he would have found her Hertfordshire neighbours had he been so unfortunate as to have made their acquaintances. Never in his wildest dreams did he suppose she was speaking of the Bennets of Longbourn. Her scheme failed miserably for, unbeknownst to her, by then he was so intent on having Elizabeth that nothing anyone might have said would change the way he felt.

Truth be told, he had known Elizabeth for scarcely a week when it became clear to him that she was the woman with whom he was destined to share his life.

Chapter 6

Blessed Time of Year

What a blessed time of year this is – my first Christmas at Pemberley. Such were Elizabeth's thoughts as she took in the fresh air. How wonderful it felt to have all her family there. Even Lydia's presence warmed her heart. Missing were her Aunt and Uncle Philips from Meryton and her Aunt and Uncle Gardiner and their adorable children. The former two, she had meant to exclude for the sake of her husband's sensibilities. He had done his best to suffer Mrs. Philips' company during the days leading up to the wedding. How Elizabeth had looked forward with delight to the time when they should be removed from her aunt's society, which was so little pleasing to Mr. Darcy or her.

As for the Gardiners and her young cousins, she picked out the brightest star in the night's sky and made a wish that they would all be together next year.

Adding to her pleasure was her Aunt Lady Vanessa's presence at Pemberley, in spite of the turmoil her ladyship had inadvertently added to their holiday party. Elizabeth knew and understood that her aunt's heart was in the right place. In the end, that was what truly mattered.

Elizabeth searched the sky for yet another star — that one perfect shining light that would make even her most improbable wish come true. Alas, it was not to be, for if she could have but one wish it would be to share that magical moment with Jane.

Darcy found Elizabeth standing outside. He too took a moment to admire the wintry landscape with the snow glistening under the night's shining stars. He knew without asking what she was thinking about — he recognised that look. She was thinking of her sister Jane.

Standing behind her, he laced his arms around her waist. She leaned into his loving embrace and rested her head against his broad chest. For the longest time, they stood there in silent wonder. Mindful of the cold air, he swept her up in his arms and carried her inside, where he commenced cradling her before the blazing fire.

Elizabeth said, "You must think me rather silly. Here I am surrounded by family and friends, and I feel sad and lonely."

"Not at all, my love."

"I feel this way every year at Christmas since losing my sister. I rather thought this year would be different, but now I am beginning to consider that I shall always feel this way at this time of year."

How it pleased her to be able to speak so openly on the subject of her sister. Prior to meeting him, expressing her thoughts in her journal had provided the means for her coming to terms with her sister's passing. Elizabeth sometimes felt that Jane's passing did not weigh as heavily upon the rest of the family. She told Darcy as much.

"I know I am not being fair, for not everyone grieves the same. I am sure my papa, my mama and my sisters are all bearing their grief as well, only in different ways."

Then again, it was Elizabeth who had refused to leave Jane's side as she waged her losing battle against what had started as a trifling cold, as her mother lamented. It was Elizabeth who held her sister in her arms as she struggled to take her last breath and ultimately gave up the fight.

Elizabeth closed her eyes to ward off her tears. She nestled closer to her husband. Meeting and falling in love with Mr. Darcy had been such a balm to her aching heart. Here was a man who understood her pain and was always there reassuring and comforting her to this day. She prayed it would always be that way.

Darcy said, "Indeed, everyone does grieve in his or her own way. As for you, my dearest, loveliest Elizabeth, you likely will suffer bouts of melancholy from time to time. That is not a bad thing. It goes to show you carry your sister in your heart forever. She will always be part of you."

Between his family and hers there existed so many shades of imperfection perfectly suitable to discord, yet when it was just the two of them like this nothing else mattered. Between Darcy and Elizabeth harmonious accord abounded. He prayed it would always be that way.

Darcy reached for one of the two glasses of rich burgundy wine that he had poured before joining his wife outside earlier and handed it to Elizabeth. At length, he took a sip of his own wine. Endeavouring to distract his wife from her sadness, he began speaking of matters that would surely lighten her spirits, for it always pleased her to laugh at the ridiculousness of others when she was certain it would not give offense. What better place than the sanctuary of their own rooms where no one would be privy to anything that was said?

Indeed, her habit had proved quite contagious and served Mr. Darcy well too. Between her sycophant cousin Mr. Collins and Darcy's aunt Lady Catherine's outrage over Pemberley's polluted shades, there was ample fodder to carry the couple for several hours until both were too exhausted for further talk, and they sought the solace of being in each other's arms in bed.

Chapter 7

Good Will and Harmony

Darcy drifted to where his sister Georgiana was standing. Placing his hand on hers, he said, "It is not too late to change your mind, you know."

"Change my mind about what?"

"I see the way you look at Wickham, especially when he is with his wife. If it troubles you to have them stay here at Pemberley, I suffer no compunction whatsoever against arranging for their stay in Lambton. Just say the words." *Please say the words,* Darcy silently prayed.

"I would be lying if I said it did not bother me a little. But Mrs. Wickham is Elizabeth's sister, and George is now her brother. I cannot expect her to choose between family loyalties merely for my sake, no matter how much I suspect you wish I might."

"I cannot dictate to you how you ought to feel, but as for myself, I shall never trust Wickham again, even if he is family."

"It means the world to me to hear you say that. You should know that regardless of the fact that it shall take some time for me to get accustomed to the idea of George's marriage, I would not trade places with Lydia for the entire world. I have you to thank that I was spared such an unenviable fate."

"Surely you must know there is nothing in the world I would not do to protect you. In time, you shall be married yourself ... sooner rather than later if our uncle has a say."

Georgiana folded one of her hands into the other. "Yes, I suspect you are correct in speaking of our uncle's favourite wish that I should soon enter the marriage market."

"Pray you will give him no mind. You are free to take as long as you wish. I hope you know how much Elizabeth and I enjoy having you live here at Pemberley with us. When the time does come for you to be married, we both will miss you exceedingly."

How uncanny it felt for Elizabeth as she reflected upon first making Lady Catherine de Bourgh's acquaintance some days ago. Where Elizabeth had expected openly displayed abhorrence, she was instead greeted with curtness and thinly disguised curiosity. Elizabeth sensed her ladyship's feigned acceptance was about to come to an end.

Indeed, having suffered feelings akin to being studied under a microscope all evening, Elizabeth braced herself for the worst upon seeing her husband's haughty aunt headed her way.

Now standing directly in front of Elizabeth, Lady Catherine said, "I suppose this is your idea of a proper family gathering, young woman."

"Indeed, your ladyship. I thank you for your kind compliment."

"Nothing in my tone conveys a measure of approbation, and you know it. I mean to test you."

Elizabeth placed her hand to her bosom. Feigning surprise, she said, "Test me, your ladyship?"

"Indeed. You ought to know, young woman, that, had I a say in the matter, you would not be standing here enjoying the privilege of being married to my nephew."

"Yes, I am well aware of your sentiments, which beg the question of your even being here."

Steadying herself, Lady Catherine's eyes narrowed. "This is what we Fitzwilliams do. Ours is a closely-knit family. Nothing, not even the pretences of an insolent little upstart the likes of you, will cause any of us to forsake years – nay, decades – old traditions."

"Lady Catherine, you need not have taken it upon yourself to educate me in the ways of your noble family, but as you have done so anyway, I am obliged to express my most heartfelt appreciation for your sacrifice."

Her ladyship narrowed her eyes. "I suppose you think you are very clever with your false words dipped in honey, but I will not be trifled with. One only needs to look at your mother, your father and your younger sisters to know you are not suited to the task of filling my dearly departed sister's shoes. I shall be keeping my eyes on you."

Elizabeth was glad to see her ladyship amble to the other side of the room and take a seat next to Lady Matlock. In a manner of speaking, she rejoiced, for now she knew for certain where Lady Catherine stood, and likewise, her ladyship knew what she might expect of Elizabeth. "So much for goodwill and harmony," Elizabeth said in a voice intended for no one in particular.

Sitting next to her sister-in-law, Lady Barrett afforded Mrs. Bennet the perfect opportunity to champion her daughters. "What a fine thing it is for my girls to have such connections," said Mrs. Bennet, "and how much finer it would be if the girls had dowries befitting the nieces of such a grand lady as yourself."

Her ladyship said nothing, which was enough to encourage Mrs. Bennet to continue her speech. "Indeed, it is my understanding that you enjoyed a handsome dowry and look how it benefited you. You attracted the notice of Sir Frederick Barrett with such a handsome dowry. One can only imagine how my Kitty and my Mary would benefit if they were similarly blessed. I know that you made Lizzy your sole beneficiary, but just look around you. What difference will your fortune make to the wife of Fitzwilliam Darcy? But for my Kitty and my Mary, a handsome dowry of twenty or thirty thousand pounds each would be the means of their marrying an earl or even a duke – at the very least a baron – instead of a physician or a law clerk. Oh, I do wish you would give the matter some thought."

Lady Vanessa said, "You *seemed* to have given

this matter a great deal of thought."

"Why, indeed I have! What else is a mother with two unmarried daughters to do? But I do think Lizzy could have given a little more consideration to the guest list for our holiday party."

"What do you mean?"

"Now that she has secured an advantageous alliance for herself, is it not her duty to place her sisters in the path of rich young men as well?"

For the sole purpose of seeing which way the conversation was going, Lady Barrett said, "There are four eligible young men in our party, and I dare say they are all handsome."

"Yes, but there are six young ladies in attendance. Besides, you might as well not count the colonel, for he is a second son, which makes him in need of a very wealthy wife. No—there are truly only three single gentlemen in our party who are really worthy of consideration. What is more, there are four unmarried ladies, all boasting of rather handsome dowries, with Miss Darcy's being the smallest at only thirty thousand pounds, but I wager Mr. Darcy is more than capable of supplementing his sister's dowry if needs be."

"I beg your pardon, but how do you know all this?"

"It is my duty to know everything about the competition if I am to stand a chance of making a match for my daughters this week."

Lady Barrett's mouth gaped. "Surely the prospect of making matches for my nieces, Mary and Kitty, is not your sole reason for being here."

"Why, of course not! Though I must say that, while I rarely find pleasure in being anywhere other than my own beloved home, Pemberley's many splendours are certainly enticing enough that I should like to spend as much time here as the rest of my years will allow. But I do not flatter myself into believing that my work is truly done until all of my daughters are well settled."

As her sister's wit continued to flow unimpeded by further interruption, her ladyship recalled why she never did care for her brother's wife. However, decades of self-imposed estrangement had taught her that accepting one's family for who and what they were was far better than facing the possibility of living life knowing that, at the end of it, there would be no one who might miss her when she was gone. Besides, her sister Bennet really was not a bad sort. Her brother might not have won the golden ticket and indeed married a woman of excellent breeding and wealth, but one look at Lady Catherine told her that such considerations mattered little in the overall scheme of things. In the end, her sister wanted the exact same thing for Kitty and Mary as she did. With that notion in mind, she set upon contemplating what part she might have in said regard, paying no attention at all to whatever topic of discussion her sister Bennet had taken up by now.

The next day, Lady Barrett wandered into the library where she saw her brother tucked away. What a magnificent room it was with rows and rows of leather-bound books stacked high towards the ornate ceiling, no doubt the collective works of several generations. Finely appointed leather chairs were strategically placed there and about to allow for one's reading pleasure. Its ambiance afforded the perfect sanctuary for the literary and the non-literary minded alike.

"I might have known I would find you here."

Mr. Bennet looked up from his book. Lowering his spectacles, he said, "Indeed. How are you this morning, my dearest sister?"

"I must say that I am happier than I have been in years. It is such a pleasure to be surrounded by all my family at Christmas. I owe much of my gratitude to you." She sat in the chair closest to her brother and placed her hands on his. With a gentle squeeze, she said, "Thank you for giving me a chance to make amends for my ill treatment of you and your wife and subsequently your lovely daughters – my nieces – all those years."

"What is done is done. Besides, we are all together now and here amidst all this splendour."

"Yes—we have come a long way from our seemingly humble beginnings in comparison to all this, have we not?"

Mr. Bennet pursed his lips. "Some of us more than others, I understand."

"Yes, it is true. I do not mean to suggest otherwise. As much as I love my nieces and I am exceedingly proud of all of them—"

Here Mr. Bennet interrupted her. "All of them? Have you met young Lydia?"

"I have no doubt that our Lydia makes herself known wherever she goes. She is wild and impetuous, but she cannot always be that way. However, what I was about to say is that one of my greatest regrets is that I never got the chance to know your eldest daughter, Jane."

Her ladyship felt her brother's hand tremble a little. She detected a gradual change in his demeanour, and never having had children of her own, she could only wonder what it must have been like for a parent to suffer the loss of a child.

After a moment, Mr. Bennet looked into his sister's eyes. "Indeed, nothing takes the place of my Jane." His eyes welled with tears. "She was all loveliness, and she never had an unkind thing to say about anyone. To Jane, the entire world was good. You would have loved her."

"Elizabeth speaks fondly of her eldest sister to this day. I imagine she always will."

"My Lizzy speaks affectionately of you as well. I owe you a great deal for taking her under your wing at a time when she needed it most."

"It is such a comfort to know that when I am no longer of this earth, all my worldly goods will be hers."

Now composed, he nodded. "You have chosen your beneficiary wisely."

"Indeed, however I want you to know that I intend to provide for all my nieces, which includes dowries of ten thousand pounds each for Mary and Kitty."

Mr. Bennet covered his mouth with his hand while he gathered his thoughts. At length, he said, "That is far too generous, and not knowing all the particulars of your situation, I do not know that I would be comfortable accepting such large sums when I ought to be the one responsible for my un-married daughters' futures."

"My estate is sizeable enough to bear such an expense with no hardship whatsoever. Besides, what is the point in being blessed with a good fortune and having no one to share it with?"

"It seems you are determined to do this, and my dear wife would never speak to me should I refuse your offer, so it seems I am obliged to say yes."

"Excellent. I shall speak with my solicitors upon my return to Bosley."

"Which of us shall have the honour of telling Mrs. Bennet?"

"I believe that is one honour I shall bestow solely upon you, dear brother."

Chapter 8

Sense of Honour

Looking across the room, Lady Catherine fumed. How was such a thing as this to be borne? A grand lady of her breeding and standing was expected to spend such a joyful time as Christmas with the likes of the people assembled in the room—tradesmen alongside the ruling class. The son of Pemberley's former steward, even her own parson claiming a connection to her family was abhorrent. *What on Earth was Darcy thinking in subjecting all of us to this travesty when he might have married my Anne?*

She threw a furtive glance his way in the hope

that his countenance bore evidence of his own abhorrence. The last she had heard, he hated George Wickham. *Is he so much in love with that wife of his that he has lost all sense of honour – forfeited his own will? Before he met that woman, he would never have spoken to more than half the people in this room. What on Earth has got into him?*

Lady Catherine was disgusted by the appalling display by Darcy's *so-called* sister as well. The wild child would have been better suited to sit quietly in a chair befitting a married woman than shamelessly flirt with her ladyship's nephew Colonel Fitzwilliam. *Such unabashed wantonness gives one to understand exactly how easily she must have succumbed to Mr. Wickham's seduction.* Her ladyship glanced across the room to where Wickham sat, embroiled in a discussion with Mr. Bennet — neither of them giving a care to restrain Mrs. Wickham. *To think that such scandalous behaviour as the Wickhams engaged in prior to their patched-up wedding is being rewarded with their presence amongst nobility.*

Not all of her nephew Darcy's new circle of acquaintances met with her ladyship's disapprobation. Elizabeth's friend from Bosley, Miss Lancaster, was indeed someone Lady Catherine could admire. The young lady had everything in her favour, which went above and beyond the fact that she was the daughter of a wealthy landed gentleman of some consequence in the world. The young lady was exceedingly attractive and amiable and she had a healthy respect for her elders. Lady Catherine was no stranger to the fact that the young woman's father's favourite wish was that his daughter would marry a Mr. Franklin Lloyd, who was from another wealthy family. Being the good daughter that she was, Miss Lancaster never opposed the idea.

Lady Catherine proceeded to afford Miss Lancaster's performance on the pianoforte the consideration it deserved; although by no means did it compare to her niece Georgiana's earlier exhibition. Lady Catherine gazed across the room to where her daughter Anne sat. *Nor does Miss Lancaster perform as well as my Anne would have had her health allowed her to apply herself.*

After a song or two, Miss Lancaster was eagerly succeeded at the instrument by Elizabeth's sister, Miss Mary Bennet. Lady Catherine recalled from the evening before just how impatient for display this Bennet daughter tended to be. She owed it to the young lady's being the plainest one in the family, surmising that music must be the one application in which the young lady endeavoured to stand out. Her performance confirmed she lacked genius as well as taste, yet she applied herself in a conceited manner suggesting a higher degree of excellence than she had indeed reached.

Music, however, was Lady Catherine's delight, and thus she sat there thinking of how much better she would have applied herself had she ever learnt to play. At the end of a long concerto, the young woman was easily persuaded by her younger sisters to play a lively tune conducive to dancing. Indeed, they were joined by two gentlemen: one being Wickham and the other being her own nephew, Colonel Fitzwilliam. Lady Catherine sat there in silent indignation that the mode of passing the evening had degenerated to this, and within minutes she relinquished the spot on the sofa near the instrument in search of more civilised diversions.

Her ladyship steeled herself as she espied Caroline Bingley coming her way. *I recall her as that little upstart who had her sights set upon Darcy. What can she possibly have to say to me?*

"Your ladyship," said Miss Bingley.

"I beg your pardon, young woman. Do I know you?"

"Pray forgive me, Lady Catherine. We met last year in town at Mr. Darcy's home."

"Ah, yes. Pray remind me, what is your name?"

"I am Miss Caroline Bingley—sister of Mr. Charles Bingley."

Lady Catherine rested one hand atop the other perched upon her walking stick. "Miss Bingley, pray what is your purpose in speaking to me?"

"If you will pardon my saying so, I sensed you

were every bit as put off by many of the members of our party as am I. I thought we might commiserate together."

Lady Catherine regarded the young woman standing before her with evident distaste. How could she not surmise that she was one of the people in the room whom her ladyship found objectionable? Why, it was widely known that the Bingley family fortune, regardless of how sizable, had been earned in trade.

"I must confess that I do indeed find it shocking – nay, an abhorrence – to meet with people who are so beneath me in consequence that it is laughable; however, I am obliged to be here at my nephew's insistence. What, pray tell, is your excuse?"

The younger woman's mouth fell open. The shocking rudeness of Lady Catherine she likened to the reception she received earlier that week from Lady Matlock as well as Lady Barrett and, yes, even Lady Holland. Did these people not know who she was? Why, she might have been the lady of the manor had that little Eliza Bennet not usurped her rightful position.

Everyone who knew anything at all about Caroline surely knew that she had fancied herself the next mistress of Pemberley. Since her arrival, she soon came to consider that it was just as well that Eliza Bennet now wore that title that might otherwise have been hers. Now Caroline had the means of becoming a future countess as soon as she decided which of the two viscounts in their party was worthy of having her.

Oh, Caroline could hardly wait until the day when she would claim her rightful place amongst high society. Lady Caroline Fitzwilliam, future countess of Matlock sounded delightful—as did Lady Caroline Holland, future countess of Bosley. She wanted nothing but to decide which of the two titles she preferred. Then she would show all of them exactly what she was about.

Before Caroline could fashion a fitting response to Lady Catherine, they were joined by Elizabeth's aunt, Lady Barrett. After the set down her ladyship had given Caroline when they were in Bosley earlier that year, owing to Caroline's unabashed disparagement of Elizabeth, she did not know whether to be pleased for the reprieve a third party afforded or further dismayed.

Chapter 9

Reason to Doubt

That morning there were but the two of them in the breakfast parlour: Lord Holland and Miss Lancaster. This circumstance indeed met with the former's pleasure. Holland was more than a little concerned about all the attention Lucy was garnering from the other gentlemen in their party. Having heard both the Fitzwilliam brothers speak of needing to marry women of fortune earlier that week, he wondered if that might be the root of their attraction to Lucy with her generous dowry of fifty thousand pounds.

"My dearest Lucy, it is such a pleasure to see you this morning. I do believe this will be our first chance to have breakfast together. You are normally a late riser."

"I am surprised you noticed, my lord."

"Oh, I noticed. I notice everything about you — as if you do not know that already." He took a sip of his coffee and continued his speech. "Indeed, this brings me to an important matter that I have been meaning to discuss with you."

"What would you like to discuss with me?"

"I mean to caution you to be wary of the gentlemen in our party whom I know to be seeking women of fortune as their future brides."

Her bright countenance turned rather chilly. "Oh, what do you care?"

"What manner of question is that? I have always wanted what is best for you. I care about *you*."

Without awaiting the footman's assistance, Lucy bolted from her chair. "I know — much like a sister."

"Lucy —"

" — Oh, leave me alone!" she shouted, throwing down her linen napkin. She headed for the door.

Holland watched in dismay as his dearest friend

raced off. What on Earth had got into her that she would speak to him in such a manner? He shook his head. *Women!*

Later that morning, Lucy found Elizabeth sitting alone in the parlour. "I was told you wished to see me," said Lucy.

"Did you speak with your father?"

"Yes, I just left him in the library. Oh, Elizabeth you will never guess what he had to say in a million years."

"I know it was urgent but pray it was not bad news."

"I suppose that all depends upon one's perspective. I can tell you that my father is quite upset by the news. I, on the other hand, could not be more pleased. Mind you, I did not let on to my father the fact that I did not share his displeasure."

"Is this something you are at liberty to discuss, for I must confess that I am more than a little intrigued by the prospect of knowing what can bring so much pleasure to one and so much displeasure to another?"

"I should like nothing more than to tell you what my father told me, but it must go no further than this room. I know I am asking a great deal of you, but you must not tell anyone, not even your husband."

"Perhaps you should not confide in me, for I cannot promise you such a thing unless it is totally immaterial to him, and then I might simply avoid bringing it up in conversation."

"I assure you Mr. Darcy will have no reason to be concerned about any of what my father told me, that is unless he has an interest in my love life, and I am rather certain he does not."

"My dear husband is bound to find out sooner or later, and then what would you have me say?"

"Let us worry about that if and when the time comes. Besides, there is no reason he should find out while we are here at Pemberley."

After much debate about the nature of Lucy's news and how it would best be handled, Lucy confided in her friend Elizabeth that her father had received word from his solicitor that the gentleman he had intended for her – Mr. Franklin Lloyd – was indeed a married man. He had secretly married a young woman of modest means in Weymouth and he had meant to keep it a secret, but he was recently found out when the elder Mr. Lloyd was made aware of his son's sizeable debts.

Hearing all this rendered Elizabeth speechless. By the time Lucy finished her account of the entire sordid affair, Elizabeth well understood why the news had met with Lucy's pleasure. Finally, Lucy was free to decide her own future marital fate.

Elizabeth took her friend by the hand. "If what you say is true, and I have no reason to doubt its veracity, why do you not wish to share the news with Lord Holland?"

Lucy jerked her hand away. "Andrew! He is the last person in the world I want to learn about Mr. Franklin Lloyd's defection."

"Why would you say such a thing? You and I both know how much you adore his lordship. Knowing that you are no longer bound by your father's wishes must certainly make a difference to him."

"I will not suffer a single moment of Andrew's pity. It is bad enough that he treats me like his younger sister. I am sure that were he privy to what Mr. Lloyd has done he might just as likely call the man out as see this outcome as a chance for the two of us to be together."

"I am rather certain you are wrong about that, Lucy."

Lucy waved her hand dismissively. "It is neither here nor there, for my father thinks it is best that no word of Mr. Lloyd's breach of trust gets out while we remain here at Pemberley." In a decidedly different tone, Lucy said, "Although nothing was truly official, the arrangement being more of a private understanding between my father and Mr. Lloyd's father, it was widely known enough for my family's reputation to be tarnished by this scandal. My father is very proud, and he will not suffer anyone's pity as a result of Mr. Lloyd's disgraceful behaviour. I am afraid Mr. Lloyd has not heard the last of this where my father is concerned."

Chapter 10

Know How to Act

After allowing Lord Robert Fitzwilliam ample opportunity to earn her esteem, owing to his obviously feigned aloofness, Caroline Bingley decided that Lord Andrew Holland would be the fortunate gentleman who might one day call her his countess. It was just as well, for Lord Holland was the more handsome of the two. Of course, Caroline and Holland had not got off to the best start when she was an honoured guest in his home. She intended to allow him to make up for any misunderstandings they suffered in the past. First, she would make him suffer, for it would not do to have him think her affections were easily bestowed.

Seeing him standing alone, she made her way across the room and stood next to him. "I seem to remember your being quite taken with a particular pair of fine eyes when we were all together in Bosley, Lord Holland."

"What do you want, Miss Bingley?"

"I merely want to congratulate you on escaping a fate that would have found you aligned with the likes of the Bennets. Surely you are aware of the scandalous behaviour of the youngest daughter, which threatened to ruin the reputation of the entire family and anyone connected to them had it not been for the patched up affair which resulted in her marriage. Your own family might have been tainted had you aligned yourself with Eliza Bennet."

"First of all, Miss Bingley, the Wickhams eloped to Gretna Green. They were not the first couple to do so, and dare I say they will not be the last."

"Were it merely as simple as that I would agree, but the truth is those two were living in sin for weeks prior to 'eloping' to Gretna Green."

Lord Holland held up his hand. "Please spare me the details."

"Do you not want to know the sort of people you are spending time with?"

"Not particularly; however, I would ask you a question."

Caroline silently congratulated herself on her success in garnering his attention as well as she did. "Ask me anything, my lord. I am yours to command."

His puzzled countenance aside, he said, "If you find the people I am spending time with so objectionable, why are you even here?"

"My acquaintance with Mr. Darcy precedes his alliance with the Bennets of Longbourn by many years. In fact, I have long been a welcomed guest here at Pemberley. I have no intention of forfeiting that right simply because Mr. Darcy chose to align himself with fools. Besides, we had every intention of being in Scarborough, but the weather impeded our plans, which, as it turns out, is most fortunate for me."

"No doubt you are most eager to elaborate."

"Indeed. Being here affords me the chance to get better acquainted with you." She looked around, and once assured of their privacy, she walked her fingers along his lapel. "I find that to be a most pleasing prospect, my lord."

Before Holland could form a fitting response, Miss Bingley's eyes gazed upward. "Oh, look, all this time you and I have been standing underneath the mistletoe," said she in an excited voice meant to garner the attention of the others in the room.

Lord Robert, who happened to be passing by, seemed especially eager to rally Holland to claim his reward from the fetching Miss Bingley. In fact, he made such a fuss that nothing would appease him other than Lord Holland's ready compliance with the long-established holiday tradition.

Wanting nothing more than to get it all over with, Holland conceded. Leaning forward, he meant to bestow a light kiss upon the young lady's cheek, but the vixen turned her head at the last second and their lips met. The contact was brief, but not brief enough to escape the notice of a particular member of their party.

Recalling how he had avoided being caught under the mistletoe with her earlier that evening, Lucy could not help being upset that Miss Bingley was the happy recipient of Lord Holland's affection. It was all she could do not to race from the room, but not wishing to call attention to herself by such a spectacle as that, she remained seated and tried to mask her hurt feelings. As if seeing Andrew kissing another woman, even in the spirit of holiday cheer, was not bad enough, she then watched as Miss Bingley laced her arm through his and proceeded to walk across the room with him in the direction of the pianoforte.

How it pained Lucy more than she wished to witness such a display. True, she had seen other women fawn over him before. It was different when she thought they had no chance for a future between them. Now things had changed — she was no longer bound by her father's dictates for her future. Of course, Lord Holland could have no way of knowing that. *Even if he knew about my changed situation, would it make a difference to the manner in which he regards me?*

As unhappy as she was with the unfolding development among Holland and Miss Bingley, there was little she could do but silently observe the disturbing familiarity that the other woman showed towards the man who truly owned her heart, even if he refused to see it for himself.

Meanwhile, Lady Barrett and her sister-in-law, Lady Clarissa Holland, took turns remarking upon the happenings all around them.

"I suspect our dear Elizabeth has a bit of matchmaking in mind," said Lady Holland.

"Do you suppose my niece is hoping one of her sisters will catch our Andrew's eye?"

"That thought never occurred to me."

"But were that indeed the case, how would you feel on the matter?"

"I would have to think about that. You know the situation with Andrew's father dictates he marries a woman of fortune."

"Indeed." That was but one of the reasons the two sisters' favourite wish had been that Elizabeth and Andrew would be married. With Elizabeth's being Lady Barrett's sole heir and with Holland's being her ladyship's nephew, the Barrett family fortune would have remained in the family as it were. Needless to say, Elizabeth had other ideas. "If not our Andrew, which lucky gentleman is the object of my niece's matchmaking schemes?"

Lady Holland said, "Oh, the gentleman is indeed my Andrew."

"And the lucky young woman is?"

"Why, Lucy, of course."

Lady Vanessa's mouth fell open. "Our Lucy! She makes no secret of her adoration for Andrew, but surely Elizabeth must know that Harvey Lancaster has other plans for his daughter's marital felicity."

"Indeed — but what do these young people care about familial obligations?"

Lady Barrett said, "It would not be a great stretch of the imagination to suppose that, were it not for Lucy's tacit engagement to a man she has not seen in years, Andrew might take notice of her."

"They are the dearest of friends—but I liken his deep affection for her being as akin to a sort of brotherly love."

"Yes—but feelings change. Many a marriage has begun without a tiny fraction of the affection that exists among those two."

"You sound as though an alliance between Andrew and Lucy would meet with your wholehearted acceptance," said Lady Clarissa.

"Our Andrew could do a great deal worse than marry the lovely Miss Lucy Lancaster. One look about this room is a testament to that."

"I know that tone, dear sister. Which of the young ladies assembled here has met with your disapprobation? No—allow me to guess." Lady Clarissa looked about the room. "Surely you do not mean Miss Darcy—she is all loveliness. I dare say she would make an excellent daughter."

"Miss Darcy is lovely indeed, but while I would not be opposed to the match, I do not imagine Andrew would take notice of her. She is rather shy and not yet out in Society."

"Is it Miss Anne de Bourgh? I know what a torment it would be for you to have to welcome her mother into our little family circle."

Lady Barrett shuddered. "Heaven forbid such a thing would ever happen. It is grave enough that I must be forced to endure her company on such occasions as this. Even that I would find more bearable than the prospect of an alliance between Andrew and the woman of whom I am thinking."

"You are not speaking of Miss Darcy, you are not speaking of Miss de Bourgh, nor are you speaking of your nieces, Miss Kitty and Miss Mary. Why that only leaves—" Lady Clarissa's mouth gaped.

"Precisely! That awful Miss Caroline Bingley. Surely you have observed how she has transferred all her ill-suited affection, so evidently reserved for Mr. Darcy when she forced herself into our company in Bosley, towards Andrew."

***

The next morning found Lady Holland and her son out and about for a stroll along one of Pemberley's fine lanes. Despite the frosty chill in the air, her ladyship was so heavily adorned in furs that she barely noticed the weather. She was on a mission to discover the inner workings of her son's heart.

First and foremost, she wanted to know how he felt about Miss Lucy Lancaster. "Pray tell me, my son, if your reservations have anything to do with the bad blood between your father and Lucy's father?"

"Mother, I do not know that I feel comfortable discussing my love life or lack thereof with you."

"Son, there is a time to be coy, and then again, there is a time when one must seize the day. You are not your father — you are nothing at all like him, and I am sure you know that Lancaster does not suffer any ill feelings towards you despite the fact that he loathes the earl. If you care for Miss Lancaster half as much as I suspect you do, then you must start behaving accordingly."

"Well, your ladyship, there is the matter of her tacit engagement with Franklin Lloyd. Have you failed to recall that I consider the gentleman a friend?"

"Ah, Mr. Franklin Lloyd — the absentee beau," she said. "The last I heard of him, he had travelled to Weymouth. Why Weymouth when he has not set foot in Bosley in years?"

"I am sure that where the gentleman spends his time is none of our concern."

"If not Lucy, then might you consider Miss Georgiana Darcy? She is everything a future countess ought to be, and I am sure Mr. Darcy would smile upon such a match for his sister."

Holland looked about to ascertain if anyone was close by and thus privy to their discourse. "Mother, please refrain yourself from such unbridled speculation!"

Lady Clarissa said, "You could do far worse than marrying young Georgiana Darcy. Speaking of marriage, I do wish you would be more guarded in your behaviour when in Miss Bingley's company."

"Your ladyship, I thought you knew me too well to suppose I might be interested in her."

His mother regarded him with circumspect. "It is not your interest in her that concerns me. She is entirely too fond of you for my taste. I am not the only person who has taken notice of it. I simply remind you to be careful where that young woman is concerned."

Lord Holland wrapped his arm about his mother's shoulder and pressed a light kiss upon her cheek. "Your admonishment is well heeded, your ladyship."

While alone in the billiards room with Darcy, Holland said, "I have the distinct impression of having been subjected to an interview by your aunt Lady Catherine this morning."

Darcy did not like the sound of that. "Does my aunt mean to measure your worth as a potential husband for my sister Georgiana?"

"I believe she views me as a prospective husband for her daughter, Miss Anne de Bourgh. Although, I would have to say that your cousin and I are safe from each other. Despite the fact that she is not the sort of woman I fancy, she has never once looked at me—even though I am quite a catch, if I must say so myself."

Preferring not to speak on the matter, Darcy sought to shift the conversation a bit. "Holland, if it has not occurred to you by now, I feel it is incumbent upon me to tell you that my lovely wife also harbours the wish of seeing you settled. She hopes for an alliance between you and Miss Lancaster."

Holland shrugged. "I am afraid this is one wish that your wife shall not receive. You do know that Miss Lancaster is all but engaged to Franklin Lloyd, do you not?"

Darcy said, "Is that a certainty? My wife does not seem to think so." *And neither does Miss Lancaster*, he thought, if he were to rely upon his wife's word as well as Miss Lancaster's behaviour.

"As you know from your own experience with your cousin, the engagement is of a peculiar nature."

"Indeed, but as you know, I never planned to satisfy my aunt and my mother's favourite wish that I should marry my cousin, and therefore I never felt particularly bound by the *arrangement*. The two of them did their part in planning the union, but its execution depended entirely upon others. Might that indeed be the case with Miss Lancaster and Franklin Lloyd?"

"I would say there is always the chance of that. However, given that Lloyd and I have been acquainted since our childhood, just as Lucy and I have, and he has even told me as recently as the last time I saw him that he indeed intended to act upon his parents' wish and ask for Lucy's hand in marriage when the time is right, I must respect his wishes."

"And how long has it been since the two of you last spoke on the matter?"

"He confirmed his intentions to me when we last spoke two years ago when he was last in Bosley, before he left for the continent."

"I would say that a great many things can happen in the span of a couple years."

"Indeed, and if Lloyd has since changed his mind, I would say that surely he would inform the Lancasters."

"What if it turns out that he no longer intends to uphold the arrangement?"

"I would be lying if I said that I did not someday wish he would do just that. Not that I would ever wish to see Lucy injured by Franklin Lloyd's defection, but I do want to see her well settled. She deserves to be happy."

"What I think you are saying is that were Miss Lancaster free of her commitment to Franklin Lloyd, you might see your way towards a more meaningful future between the two of you."

"Trust me, my friend. Were I to learn that Lucy is no longer bound by her father's arrangement, I would know how to act."

Chapter 11

The Institution of Marriage

Darcy was beginning to feel that there was nowhere in his own home that he might escape the Wickhams. How was it that they always managed to be in the breakfast room whenever he was there? He consulted his mental calendar. *In less than a week, I shall see the back of them for what I hope will be a long, long while.*

Young Lydia, who had been in the midst of regaling those gathered at the breakfast table with accounts of their adventures in Gretna Green when Darcy walked into the room, continued where she left off.

George Wickham cleared his throat. "I am rather certain that Darcy would not wish to discuss any of that at present, Mrs. Wickham. There is a time and place for such talk, and now is neither of the two."

Darcy rolled his eyes. The last thing he wanted was that vile man speaking for him — even if he did speak the truth. His wife's youngest sister had not changed one bit from the time he first saw her at that run-down building. Wickham, on the other hand, was putting forth a valiant attempt to convince everyone that he was indeed a better man than the one who had stolen off with the youngest Bennet daughter and who had fornicated with her for weeks before finally marrying her in Gretna Green under the threat of facing a long stint in debtor's prison.

Lydia said, "Surely even Mr. Darcy will not mind my telling everyone what fun we had once we got to Scotland. Although, I did not suffer any fun at all on the journey being forced to travel in the carriage with that horrid Mrs. Shaw while my Wickham and Mr. Darcy travelled in Mr. Darcy's large barouche..."

"Who is Mrs. Shaw?" asked Kitty, her face beaming with curiosity.

"Oh, she was that horrible woman that Mr. Darcy forced me to stay with after he found me and my Wickham — "

Mr. Collins, who had been silent through it all, nodded his head as if in silent prayer. Even Bingley's brother-in-law, the indolent Mr. Hurst, who lived only to eat, drink, and play at cards, looked up from his plate laden with meat and eggs and regarded *poor* Mr. Darcy with a look of sympathy.

Wickham's colour heightened, hints of his old self crept into his voice. "Mrs. Wickham!"

She covered her mouth. "Oh, but I should not have said a word about all that. But then again, what would be the harm in my saying anything now that we are married?"

An uncomfortable silence fell over the room. All eyes were on the newlyweds. George Wickham stood. "Mrs. Wickham, I insist you join me in our apartments."

"La! Is it not rather early in the morning for us to be retiring to our rooms? But I suppose if you insist, I should like that very much."

By now, more than one face in the room had taken on a bright shade of crimson. Darcy was thankful that his wife and his sister Georgiana were not in the room to bear witness to such a vulgar spectacle.

Wickham's patience faded. "I insist!"

Shortly thereafter, the other guests began taking

their leave and soon only Darcy and Miss Caroline Bingley remained. She picked up her cup and moved to a chair closest to his. He braced himself.

"Mr. Darcy, I can only imagine how you must be suffering this week with all your new Bennet acquaintances. I suppose you are secretly kicking yourself by now. You cannot say I did not warn you."

Darcy said, "What are you talking about, Miss Bingley?"

"You will recall how I attempted to warn you about *your* precious Eliza's family when we were all in Bosley."

Of course he remembered. Miss Bingley's duplicity had served as the final nail in the proverbial coffin as regarded his esteem for her. Darcy said nothing.

"Had you heeded my warning, you most certainly would not now be forced to endure the company of the man who would be your worst enemy. Your own father's steward now proudly boasts of being your brother. How do you endure it?"

As she prattled on, Darcy recalled his earlier sentiments that he would rather endure Miss Bingley's company than Wickham's any day of the week. He was quickly beginning to have second thoughts.

"Oh, and what a charming mother-in-law you have. I do recall her saying how nothing would please her more than to remain here at Pemberley with you for the rest of her days."

Finishing his cup of coffee, Darcy listened to her with perfect indifference while she chose to entertain herself in this manner. As his composure convinced her that all was safe, her wit flowed long.

Wickham took his wife by the arm as soon as they were alone and threw her on her bed. She giggled and without being prompted assumed a most unladylike pose. "It looks like I have been a very naughty girl who is about to be punished."

"This is not a game, Lydia. You know I mean to make a good impression upon Darcy and Lady Barrett this week so I might prevail upon them to make my fortune."

"Oh, but you have not changed a bit, have you, my dear Wickham? You and I are both so very wicked."

"That self-righteous arse Darcy and your obscenely rich aunt do not need to know that, do they? All you need to do is pretend that you have changed as well. Persuade the two of them that you, too, are deserving of something more than the meagre scraps that Mrs. Darcy manages to send when she is of a mind to be charitable."

"Oh, Wickham, you know I would do anything to please you. And I have tried, I really have. And now I insist that you do your part in *pleasing* me."

"For heaven's sake, Lydia. What do you expect of me? I am not a machine!"

She pouted. "Am I to blame for longing to suffer your ardent desire for me morning, night and day?" she said as she began unfastening the flap of his trousers. "Pray allow little Wickham to come out and play. Besides, big Wickham interrupted my breakfast. I am famished. If I cannot have food to satisfy my hunger, I must have this."

She commenced doing all the things that promised to give rise to his ardour and within minutes all reason threatened to escape him. He had to admit one thing about his eager young bride: no other woman satisfied him half as much as she did, not the older, worldlier servant he had sneaked off with the night before or the comely scullery maid he had taken the day before that. Here with his wife is where he truly wanted to be. His scheme to ingratiate himself with that pompous Darcy could wait.

Darcy closed his book and allowed his eyes to rest upon his wife. Colonel Fitzwilliam, who sat next to him, leaned closer and spoke in a hushed tone. "You are no doubt thinking how pleased you will be when all your guests are away and your home returns to some sense of normalcy."

"On the contrary, my friend. I am rather thinking what a wonderful thing the institution of marriage is."

"You really do love her."

"With all my heart and soul," said Darcy, his eyes still trained on his lovely wife.

"I recall a time when you considered horse-racing your greatest passion."

Darcy looked at his cousin incredulously. "Your point being?"

"It has been months since you last took an active interest in horse racing. When are you planning to take over the reins of your budding empire once again?"

Lord Matlock, who also sat close by, could not resist chiming in. "My son makes a valid point, Darcy. Horse-racing is in your blood. It defies reason that you continue to neglect your sport."

"You both know my feelings on the matter — all in due time. My first priority is my wife and our life here at Pemberley."

The manner of his avowal must have been encouraging. "It pleases me to know that all will be as it ever was — in due time," said Lord Matlock.

Darcy hesitated a few seconds. "I would not go so far as to state it in such a manner as that, my lord."

Half smiling, Colonel Fitzwilliam said, "Yes — but you will." Emboldened, he went on to speak of his ideas for the upcoming racing season, and as much as Darcy would have liked to pretend otherwise, his interest was piqued. Before long, the three gentlemen made their way to Darcy's stables to carry on their rather lively discussion with his head groom.

Chapter 12

My Brother's Keeper

Later that day, Darcy was displeased when George Wickham waltzed into the room. His voiced laced with disdain, Darcy said, "Did I not tell you to keep your distance from me? How dare you come into my study in a manner suggesting you own the place?"

"Darcy, I heard you speaking to Lord Matlock and that idiot Colonel Fitzwilliam about the coming races in the spring. I have a proposition to make, one that will be lucrative for all of us, if you are interested."

It was all Darcy could do not to laugh aloud.

"That you would believe I am interested in anything you have to say is a clear indication that you have lost your mind."

Not to be put off so easily as that, George Wickham said, "Now that we are brothers, I had hoped we could put our differences aside. I was especially optimistic when my dear Lydia told me that we were to spend Christmas time at Pemberley. I cannot tell you how much I missed this place. Indeed, I shall forever remember Pemberley as my own home. It is certainly the only home I have ever known. I should hope that one day my children will run and play amongst these halls with your children the same as you and I once did."

Darcy, having remained silent long enough while that fool rambled on, said, "You must certainly know that you are the last man in the world I ever expected to see here at Pemberley. I certainly did not invite you into my home. You have your *dear* wife to thank for insinuating herself into Lady Barrett's good graces as your sole reason for being here."

Darcy leaned forward in his chair. "As for your children one day playing alongside *my* children, I would not count on that if I were you."

Wickham laughed. "Do you think for one minute that *your* dear wife would turn her back on her own sister — her own flesh and blood?"

Rock hard self-control is what the moment dictated. "You think you have this all figured out."

"Indeed, we are, after all, one big, happy family. By the bye, I must not forget to thank your lovely wife for regularly advancing the funds to see that my wife does not want for many of the finer things that are not always available to her on the pay of a mere commissioned officer."

If Wickham's intention had been to nettle Darcy, then he surely succeeded with that last remark. Darcy was livid over the thought that Elizabeth might be a party to what Wickham suggested.

A quarter hour later, Darcy stormed into his wife's room, where she was attending a rather large floral arrangement, and marched straight to the window. After taking deep breaths as if trying to calm himself, he finally spoke. "Have I told you lately how much I loathe George Wickham?"

Sorting out several sprigs, Elizabeth said, "Oh, dear. What has my brother done to upset you now?"

Darcy tore his eyes away from the window and regarded his wife with heightened dismay. "*Must* you refer to that wretched man as your brother?"

"I suppose I might cease referring to Wickham as such, but that does not change the fact that he is indeed my brother. I believe he is your brother as well."

"And I am to be my brother's keeper?"

"What does that mean?"

"You ought to know — that is, if what that wretch said is true."

Elizabeth laid the sprigs aside. "What did Wickham say?"

"He said that you regularly supply your sister with funds."

"I would have to say I am guilty as charged."

Darcy ran his fingers through his hair. "How much? How often?"

"Well, I would not say that I have given my sister anything close to the three or four hundred a year she has requested. That being said, such relief as it is in my power to afford by the practice of diligent economy in my own private expenses, I frequently send them."

"Elizabeth, you must stop! You know how much I abhor that vile man. Having spent upwards of ten thousand pounds to set him upon his current situation surely you can understand how I would not wish to see another shilling go his way."

"What would you have me do? It is evident that such an income as theirs, under the direction of two people so extravagant in their wants and heedless of the future, must be very insufficient. I am not up to the task of turning my back on a sister in need."

Fearing that this matter might prove to be a lasting source of quarrel between him and his wife, Darcy said, "Lady Barrett has expressed an interest in getting to know her niece better. What finer way than to begin subsidising her manner of living?"

"You cannot be serious!"

"The knowledge that Wickham is still benefiting from my financial largess changes everything. I will not be a party to it. What is more, I want him gone."

"Well, as Lady Vanessa is the one who invited him into our home, I would say he is her guest. When she goes, he and my sister Lydia should go as well."

"It is as it should be and in order to leave nothing to chance, I think I shall speak to her on the matter."

Elizabeth walked behind her husband and placed her hands on his shoulders. He was stiff as could be, which could not be a good thing. She said, "Come have a seat on the bed."

"You know it is not in my nature to refuse such a tempting request from you, my lovely wife, but I mean to speak with your aunt as soon as can be. I do not want to allow for any more misunderstandings as far as the Wickhams are concerned."

"What I have in mind shall not take very long, and I promise by the time I have had my way with you, you will be thanking me."

"I do like the sound of that. Perhaps you might show me what you have in mind."

When he sat, Elizabeth stood directly in front of him in between his legs and commenced lowering his jacket from his shoulders. When she was done, she folded it neatly over her arm and then laid it aside. Then she joined him on the bed, moved directly behind him and placed her hands on either of his shoulders. Rubbing and massaging, she leaned closer and spoke softly in his ear. "Do you like this?"

"I do, although I did think you had something else on your mind — something that required far less clothing."

"Try to enjoy this and, if you will give me leave, I shall endeavour to engage in more pleasurable activities later tonight."

Many of the younger adults later found themselves all together in the blue parlour. Miss Caroline Bingley, in her continuing bid to garner Lord Holland's attention, walked about the room fully aware that it was the ideal manner in which to display her figure to its fullest advantage. Elizabeth sat next to her dear friends Lucy and Charlotte and merely contented herself with the spectacle of it all.

It was all well and good until Caroline upped the stakes by calling on Holland directly to join her for a walk about the room. His being ever the consummate gentleman likely prompted his ready acceptance, much to Lucy's dismay.

Having spoken to her friend earlier that evening on the subject of Lord Holland's increasing forbearance of Miss Bingley of late, when he barely tolerated her when she descended upon his home in Bosley, Elizabeth was well aware that Lucy feared Lord Holland had succumbed to the other woman's charms. As much as Lucy did not like the unfolding development, she felt it was beyond her power to do anything about it. Lord Holland was free to choose where he would, even if it meant not choosing her. Her friendship with him had never given her licence to criticise the women who threw themselves in his path before. As Lucy was determined to keep the news of Mr. Lloyd's defection a secret from Pemberley's guests at the request of her father for the sake of his family's wounded pride, why should it now?

Elizabeth had not wanted to believe such a change in attitude was possible; however, Holland's actions towards Miss Bingley of late rendered Lucy's assertions difficult to refute. Elizabeth began to suppose she did not know Lord Holland half as well as she thought she did.

Miss Bingley said, "There is nothing like a leisurely walk about the room after having tea. Although I am certain that, were it not for the cold Derbyshire weather, I should like it very much were you and I to enjoy a leisurely stroll out of doors, Lord Holland."

She looked at Elizabeth. "I am rather certain the weather outside has done nothing at all to dampen your enthusiasm for walking outdoors, dearest Eliza. I do recall your being an excellent walker when you resided in Hertfordshire."

"Indeed, I have always enjoyed the solace a long walk affords, even on a cold winter's day."

"I have always been given to believe that engaging in such an endeavour reflects an abominable sort of conceited independence, a most country-town indifference to decorum."

Darcy was so much irritated by Miss Bingley's intended slight as to leave him very little attention for his book. Laying it wholly aside, he said, "You are certainly entitled to your opinion on the matter, Miss Bingley, but I tend to disagree. As for my wife's wont of taking long walks, in particular, it reflects an adventurous spirit that is not constrained by the dictates of society. It is but one of an exceedingly long list of things I find most appealing."

"But of course, Mr. Darcy. By no means did I aim to disparage your lovely wife. I was merely speaking in generalities. Pray you took no offence, dearest Eliza."

"No one who truly knows you can be offended by anything you say, dearest Caroline."

A short pause followed this speech before Miss Bingley began again by taking up a conversation about books, specifically the size of her brother's collection as compared with Darcy's.

"I am astonished," said Miss Bingley, "that my father should have left so small a collection of books. What a delightful library you have at Pemberley, Mr. Darcy!"

"It ought to be good. It has been the work of many generations," said Darcy, his annoyance with the lady still evidenced by his tone.

"And then you have added so much to it yourself. You are always buying books."

"I cannot comprehend the neglect of a family library in such days as these."

"Neglect!" Miss Bingley cried, her eyes sweeping about the room. "I am sure you neglect nothing that can add to the beauties of this noble place. Charles, when you build your house, I wish it may be half as delightful as Pemberley." In a bid to flatter her companion, whom she now sat next to on the settee, she said, "I should be just as pleased were it half as delightful as Avondale as well." In a show of affection that seemed somewhat out of place, she placed her hand on Holland's. "Have I told you how much I adore your home, my lord?"

"I believe you mentioned your adoration on several occasions, Miss Bingley."

"Upon my word, Caroline," said her brother Charles, "I should think it more possible to get either Pemberley or Avondale by purchase than by imitation."

Holland shrugged. "Were it not for the entail, I wager *the earl*," he said, his voice denoting its usual disdain when speaking of his father, "would sell Avondale to you in under a heartbeat, Bingley, especially if I am to judge by the rapid depletion of my family's stock of thoroughbreds."

Colonel Fitzwilliam, who walked into the parlour in time to hear the end of Holland's speech, insisted upon having his share of the conversation. "I was not aware that the earl had offered additional thoroughbreds for sale." He turned to Darcy. "Were you aware of this?"

Darcy, having returned his attention to his book, set it aside and responded to his cousin that indeed he was. And with that the conversation moved decidedly in the direction of horses, much to Miss Bingley's dismay, for try as she might to pretend otherwise, her knowledge of horses was paltry at best.

Chapter 13

Anything in His Power

Darcy nuzzled the back of his lovely wife's long, slender neckline. This was the best Christmas Eve morning ever. *Nothing feels better than being with the woman I love on such a fine morning as this.* He chuckled, well aware that he would be professing a similar sentiment on Christmas morning. Knowing the better part of Christmas Day would be spent in church, as well as surrounded by their family and friends, Darcy made plans for a special early morning escape with his wife. She stirred and slowly turned to face him. He spoke softly. "Good morning, my love."

Elizabeth smiled. "Good morning." She looked about the room. "What time is it?"

Darcy said, "It is early—very early I am afraid. I fear I have never been able to sleep late on Christmas Eve morning. What say you we go out for an early morning ride—just the two of us before the rest of the household begins to stir? If we hurry, we will catch the sunrise. Would that not be lovely?"

Elizabeth trailed her finger along his chiselled jaw. "You surprise me, my love. I thought surely you would have other endeavours in mind for our first Christmas Eve morning as man and wife."

Darcy pressed his lips against his teasing wife's. "If you insist, I suppose we might delay our outdoor adventure by just a few minutes."

Elizabeth laughed. "A few minutes you say. That hardly sounds promising."

His dark eyes filled with adoration. "You would be amazed."

Not too long afterwards, Darcy and Elizabeth raced down the stairs on their way to the stables for their early morning escape with the excitement of children.

Lucy, who was not known to be an early riser, startled them. "Where are the two of you off to in such a hurry on this rather fine morning?"

"My wife and I are on our way to the stables."

"Yes, I understand my dear husband has planned a surprise for me."

Mr. Collins appeared from nowhere. He bowed. "Pardon me, Mr. Darcy, Mrs. Darcy. I do not mean to intrude upon your pleasure, but I could not help overhearing that you are on your way to the stables. I am not unaware, sir, that you are the proud owner of some of the finest bays in all of England. I should very much like to accompany you and see them for myself."

Elizabeth said, "I did not think you had an interest in horse racing, sir."

"Though I do not seek to profit from the sport, I am obliged to confess my ardent interest. I fancy myself quite the connoisseur of fine horse flesh." Here he coloured and said, "Which is not to suggest that I do anything other than admire them, sir—"

Darcy held up his hand. "Sir, I know precisely what you mean. I would be happy to give you a private tour, but—"

Next thing, Lord Holland rounded the corner. "Why don't we all have a tour?"

Frustrated, Darcy said, "What a fine idea, Holland. Shall we invite the entire household?"

Espying her friend Charlotte descending the stairs, Elizabeth said, "There is no need for all that. What say you we make this a party of six? Lucy,

Charlotte? Would you like a tour of Mr. Darcy's stables as well? Who among us is not impressed with fine horse flesh?"

Both ladies' smiles signalled their willingness and not long thereafter their little party was bundled in coats and scarfs, gloves and mittens, and fur bonnets and hats, on their way to the stables.

Attempting to replace her husband's dour countenance with a smile, Elizabeth laced her arm through his and rested her head on his chest. "Why the forlorn look, Mr. Darcy?"

"I meant to spend this morning alone with you, my love."

"I know you did, but this is so much better — being surrounded by such dear friends. Soon, they will be gone, and then it will be just the two of us — save Georgiana."

When they arrived at the stables, everyone was in awe of the spectacle before them — a wonderfully decorated open sleigh with four festively adorned horses.

Elizabeth bestowed a loving, somewhat apologetic smile towards her husband and silently voiced, "Thank you." He sheepishly accepted her gratitude.

Rather than take turns enjoying a jaunt about the park, they all crowded into the sleigh which, as it turned out, accommodated them quite nicely with

Darcy, Elizabeth and Charlotte seated on one row and Holland, Lucy, and Collins on the other. As the driver set off along a wintry path lined on either side with snow covered pines, Lucy commenced regaling Charlotte with an account of Holland's exploits when she, Elizabeth, Darcy and Holland were together in Bosley. Holland simply laughed at his dear friend's teasing as she playfully chastised him for putting on such a perilous exhibition.

They could laugh about it now, but it was surely no laughing matter at the time. The sight of the viscount lying on the ground with his head swimming in a pool of his own blood was a spectacle they were likely never to forget. Elizabeth could recall only one time before when she had been so terrified by the prospect of losing someone that she cared about. At that moment, she felt the touch of her husband's hand on hers.

Darcy gently squeezed his wife's hand when they spoke of how they had spent the better part of the night fearing that Holland might not recover from his fall. That experience had been the means of her sharing her heartrending story about her sister Jane's tragic death. They hardly knew each other, and yet she had opened up to him so freely.

Their eyes met. Whatever the rest of their party was speaking of during the moment was lost to him. All he could do was think about how much he adored this woman and how he would do anything in his power to make her happy. He silently voiced, "I love you."

Chapter 14

A Thousand Times

Despite the lovely morning they all enjoyed, Elizabeth was growing increasingly concerned that Lucy and Holland were no closer to declaring their undying love for each other than when they first arrived at Pemberley. What a shame, for if ever two people belonged together, it was those two. Between her friend Lucy and his lordship there existed every possible symptom of love.

Something had to change. There sat Holland on one side of the room and there sat Lucy on the other.

They may as well have been on opposite sides of the world.

Elizabeth watched in dismay as Miss Bingley pranced over to where Holland stood and commenced cajoling him to have a turn about the room with her. If Elizabeth could change but one thing about her holiday party, it would be Miss Bingley's being there. *What an unexpected ripple in my plan.* What had started as a brief respite at Pemberley to allow Miss Bingley to recuperate from her ailment had resulted in an extended stay. To the Bingleys' credit, adverse weather conditions had been a factor in the decision for them to stay at Pemberley rather than risk journeying on to Scarborough.

Still, it would have been so much better if Miss Bingley were less flagrant in her attempts to ensnare Holland with her arts and allurements. Elizabeth shook her head. Either he was totally oblivious of her scheme, or he was actually attracted to the woman.

By now, the two were once again standing beneath the mistletoe. Elizabeth rolled her eyes at the prospect of yet another spectacle. The next thing she knew, her friend Lucy raced from the room.

Enough is enough! Elizabeth marched across the floor to where Holland and Miss Bingley stood. "Lord Holland, I would like a word with you." Elizabeth looked at his astonished companion. "In private." Lacing her arm through his, Elizabeth led Holland into an adjacent room and closed the door.

Turning to face him, she folded one arm over the other. "I hope you are proud of yourself."

By now, his countenance reflected a measure of astonishment equal to his former companion's. "Pardon?"

"I am rather certain you heard me."

"What did I do?"

"It is more of a case of what you did not do."

"Whatever it is that you are accusing me of, you had better come right out and say."

"Why do you simply allow the likes of Miss Bingley to fawn all over you in such an appalling manner?"

"I beg your pardon, *Mrs. Darcy*. I believe you forfeited any right to advise me on my love life long ago."

Elizabeth winced. She could scarcely believe he was bringing up her aunt's scheme for the two of them to be married at such a time as this. Both of them had accepted that such an alliance was not meant to be. Rather than allow his retort to hinder her from her purposes, she said, "So, you are in love with her?"

"I think you know me better than that."

"I thought I knew you, sir. I always supposed you and Lucy would find your way to each other."

"I have made no secret of my deep affection for Miss Lancaster, but as you and I both know, she is promised to another."

If ever there was a time to break a confidence this was it. "Then you mean to say you have not heard?"

"Heard what?"

"Mr. Lloyd is married to a young woman who resides in Weymouth."

His eyes opened wide. "Lucy must be devastated." He ran his fingers through his hair. "She said nothing of any of this to me."

"Perhaps she was not at liberty to say anything."

"Not even to me?"

"The last thing she wants is anyone's pity."

"But she and I have always been close. In fact—" The dawn of recognition spread over his countenance. "Lucy is no longer under any obligation ... she is free to marry where she will."

As if oblivious of the cold as well as the fact that she had raced outside without bothering to don her coat, Lucy paced the balcony. "Who am I fooling? Andrew does not even know I am alive when it comes to regarding me as other than a sister." As she was talking aloud to herself, she was startled upon learning she was no longer alone.

"Merry Christmas."

Having been startled initially by the sound of his melodious voice, as well as secretly pleased if she were forced to admit the truth, his being there also quickly reminded Lucy of her annoyance with him. "What do you want, my lord?"

"What sort of question is that? I saw you leave the room. I came to see what was the matter."

"I am surprised you managed to tear yourself away from Miss Bingley."

"It is not like you to be jealous."

"How do you know what I am like?"

"You are upset with me. No — do not deny it," he said playfully.

Lucy was hardly in the mood for humour. She said nothing.

Lord Holland said, "Allow me to make amends." By now, he was standing directly in front of her—taunting her, she supposed. He placed his fingers under her chin and tenderly coaxed her to look him directly into his eyes: dark, alluring eyes. "Will you grant me a favour?"

"I do not suppose it is within my power to deny you anything. What do you have in mind?"

He raised his other hand above her head and in so doing piqued Lucy's curiosity. She looked up and saw the sprig of mistletoe dangling above. Before she knew what he was about, the touch of his lips upon hers made everything else around her fade. He had kissed her hand a thousand times before, so she surely knew the sensation of his lips upon her skin.

His soft, moistened lips upon hers evoked in her feelings akin to nothing she had ever felt before; something warm and enticing, tender and undemanding—near mystical. She likened Lord Holland's lips to the sweetest thing she ever tasted in her life. This was one moment she wished never to end.

A frission of panic overcame her and all too soon she was given to know they were not alone when the familiar sound of her father clearing his throat shattered the bliss-filled silence.

"What is the meaning of this?" Mr. Lancaster demanded.

Lucy pushed herself away from his lordship. "Father, you misunderstand, Andrew — I mean to say Lord Holland and I were merely honouring the tradition of —" Her voice cracked. "It was the mistletoe."

"What mistletoe?"

Her heart stumbled before once again finding its rhythm. She looked at her companion pleadingly. "Tell him, Lord Holland."

Holland flashed his open palms. "What mistletoe?"

His arms crossed, his temper flaring, Mr. Lancaster glared at the younger man. "You owe me an explanation, sir."

"Indeed, I do and if you will allow me a few moments more alone with your daughter, I shall seek your private audience immediately thereafter. It seems I have something of great urgency to discuss with your daughter that is long overdue."

"You have five minutes!"

After Mr. Lancaster stormed off, Lucy said, "What are you doing, Andrew? Do you know what you are about?"

"Lucy, I am sorry that I took as long as I did to act upon the tender feelings I have for you, but I never wanted to cause a rift between you and your parents. I know I have never been your father's favourite person owing to his fierce dislike of my father, which is hardly an excuse for not telling you how much you mean to me before now, but there is also the matter of your father's intention for you to marry Mr. Franklin Lloyd."

"What are you saying?"

"Marry me," he said. "Rather, please do me the honour of accepting my hand. Come live with me at Avondale and be my future countess."

Lucy pinched herself. She pinched him.

"What are you doing?"

"I wanted to make sure I was not dreaming."

Rubbing his arm, he said, "Then, why did you pinch *me*?"

"I wanted to make certain that you were real—that it is really you, Lord Andrew Holland, the only man in the world that I have ever truly desired, standing here and offering your hand in marriage."

He took both her hands in his and drew one and then the other to his lips. "I am very real and I am waiting on your reply. Will you be my bride?"

She shook her head. She cried, "Yes, yes, a thousand times yes."

He pulled her in his arms and commenced showing her the strength of his desire for her. Finally enjoying the freedom to kiss the woman who owned his heart in such a manner as this took his breath away and filled his body with longing. This woman, who, unbeknownst to her, had driven him to distraction for years, was truly his. He thought about taking his jacket off and wrapping it around her shoulders and then taking her by the hand and leading her down the stone stairs so that they might enjoy a lovely stroll hand in hand along the lane before making their way back inside to share their joy with the other guests.

First, he needed to secure her father's permission and ideally his blessing. Then they would be free to shout it out to the world that he, Lord Andrew Holland, and Miss Lucy Lancaster were to be married.

"Shall we return inside the house where it is nice and warm? I find I can hardly wait to speak with your father."

"I have waited all these years with one wish that you would notice me and it turns out that you have."

"Indeed. I have noticed you. You mean the world to me—you always have."

"You do not know what it means to me to hear you say those words. May we not have just a few minutes more before we join the others?"

"I would say yes, except that it is terribly cold out here, and I would not have you catch your death of cold."

Lucy stretched out her arms and whirled around. "Is it cold? I cannot feel anything but joy and happiness and warmth."

Here Holland did take his coat off and wrapped it about her shoulders. "Indeed, it is cold out here."

"I really do not care. I no longer have a care in the world."

"I care." He kissed her lightly upon her cheek. "Come inside while I speak with your father. Then later this evening, when the house is settled, we shall meet here for a lovely moonlit stroll. Agreed?"

"Whatever you say, my lord, for I am yours to command."

"Ah, I shall remember that when you and I are man and wife."

Chapter 15

Between Now and Then

The Bingley party comprised the first wave of guests to take their leave of Pemberley. Charles Bingley wisely elected to remove his family the day after the heavily anticipated post-Christmas Day fox hunt, for by then his sister's anger over Lord Holland's defection had threatened to boil over into a most embarrassing spectacle. Indeed, upon realizing her best laid plans to be the future mistress of Avondale were all for naught, she was livid. In seeking solace for her bruised vanity, she blamed Mrs. Darcy for her interference. How could she do otherwise? The timing between Eliza's rude interruption of

Caroline's last stint under the mistletoe with the dashing viscount and the announcement of his engagement to Miss Lancaster was too uncanny for her to suppose otherwise.

The Fitzwilliams said their goodbyes next. Lady Catherine, having enjoyed no luck at all in making a match between Anne and either of her single cousins, decided to continue her campaign in Matlock where she planned to remain until her brother and sister, Lord and Lady Matlock, travelled to London for the seating of Parliament, as well as the Matlocks' Twelfth Night ball.

The Collinses travelled to Hertfordshire with the Bennet party in order that Charlotte might spend time at Lucas Lodge with her family before returning to Hunsford. Mr. Collins was thankful that his noble patroness had blessed the visit, even though she did remind him that his duties to his parishioners had best not be neglected for long.

The Wickhams were invited to spend as much time as they desired at Barrington Hall with Lady Barrett, an invitation that satisfied the newlyweds' favourite wishes immensely. Elizabeth prayed her aunt would not come to regret her decision where those two were concerned, even as she suspected that Wickham and Lydia would still be in Bosley when she and Darcy arrived six months hence for Lucy and Holland's wedding.

All that remained were the Lancasters and Lord Holland, who, after having received Mr. Lancaster's blessing (albeit with more reserve than one might expect of a father whose only daughter was about to marry a viscount), decided he did not wish to be separated for even a day from his newly betrothed.

Elizabeth and Lucy sat in the parlour on the morning of the Lancasters' leave taking from Pemberley. The long engagement period was the topic at hand.

"I believe my father thinks that I shall overcome my so-*called* infatuation with Andrew if given another Season in town," said Lucy. "Clearly he does not know me at all to even suppose such a thing."

"One would imagine that your father would be thrilled about your pending nuptials and your being a future countess in due time."

"I think he would, were it anyone but Andrew to whom I was to be married."

"I rather supposed your father was particularly fond of Lord Holland. Until recently, I never detected a hint of his ill-will towards the viscount."

"It is not the viscount, but rather his father, the earl, Lord Lawrence Holland, whom my father objects to. There has always been bad blood between them. I think it has to do with the earl's interest in my mother before she and my father were married, but as I know none of the particulars, I am not at liberty to say more, and you must not repeat a word of what I have said to you to anyone. I have long considered my father's low opinion of Andrew's father to be none of my concern and I have told him so."

"What an uncharitable speech. I always supposed you were hesitant to say or do anything that did not meet with your father's approbation. Bravo!" said Elizabeth.

"I shall attribute my new found bravado where my excellent father is concerned to you, Elizabeth. I feel compelled to say the way you managed all your disparate guests over the past week was nothing short of masterful. Did I not see you and the formidable Lady Catherine de Bourgh embracing prior to her leave taking?"

"I would say the exhibition required a great deal of rather clever acting on both our parts. And just think, I am to endure her company for weeks in Kent this Easter, when Mr. Darcy makes his annual pilgrimage to visit her."

"I do hope you and Mr. Darcy will be once again in London before the height of the Season."

"Indeed, I am hoping for many chances for the two of us to enjoy each other's company before Fitzwilliam and I join you in Bosley in the summer for your wedding."

"Indeed. I truly look forward to the Matlocks' Twelfth Night ball."

"As do I, to be sure. As you know, this will be my first Season in town. I am all anticipation."

"And just imagine how much fun we will have—you and Mr. Darcy and Andrew and me. We will be the envy of everyone everywhere we go, I am quite convinced."

Darcy handed Elizabeth down from the open sleigh—the same one they had all crowded into days earlier on Christmas Eve. Neither of them would have exchanged the joyous time spent with friends and family alike, but at last all their guests were gone. This was their time.

Hand in hand, they walked up the pathway leading to a small, unremarkable cabin tucked away in the woods. Darcy opened the door and stepped aside to allow his wife to enter before him. She felt as though she had stepped inside a magical room—one awash in candlelight. A roaring fire in keeping with the season added to the room's allure, as did the sound of music emanating from one of the adjoining rooms.

Such a wonderful scene as that which she beheld took her breath away. She placed her hand to her bosom. "What is all this?"

"This is the surprise I had planned for you on Christmas Eve morning."

Darcy commenced helping Elizabeth take off her coat. Her spirits quickly rose to playfulness. "I believe the others would have appreciated your surprise too," she said, her eyes beaming and her voice teasing.

"On the contrary, my love, this is meant to be a romantic refuge for two."

After removing and securing his own coat, Darcy took his wife by her hand and led her into a small breakfast parlour. A footman was in the corner playing a violin, which explained the music. Another stood by the sideboard that was laden with food.

Darcy escorted Elizabeth to the table and assisted her into her seat. "Allow me the pleasure of preparing a plate of your favourite foods."

In a voice of wonder, Elizabeth said, "I am starting to feel so very special. To what do I owe such thoughtful consideration?"

"I watched and admired your ability to handle not only your family, but my family as well, with all the charm and grace befitting the mistress of Pemberley. It has not been very easy, especially having to endure my aunt Lady Catherine, as well as Miss Bingley." Paying no mind to the servants in the room, he took her hand and raised it to his lips. "I could not be more proud of you, my dearest, loveliest Elizabeth."

Hours later, she fondly recollected the last time she lay in her husband's arms in the middle of the day. It was during the earliest days of their marriage when the two of them were getting to know each other as man and wife. Other than dedicate themselves to said cause, the two of them behaved as though they did not have a care in the world. It was all the two of them could do to keep their hands from each other. A frisson of delight coursed through her body in remembrance of those times. She brushed her hand across Darcy's bare chest and commenced tracing the pattern of his neckline and the lines of his chin with her fingers.

He opened his eyes. "I thought you were asleep, my love."

"No—I am awake."

"Are you ready to return to the manor house?"

"No, I am not, unless you have pressing matters to attend to, and then I suppose we ought to return. Your sister may start to wonder what has become of us."

"Mrs. Reynolds is fully aware of our plans. She will inform Georgiana should she ask about us."

Elizabeth smiled knowingly. Of course, Mrs. Reynolds would take care of such matters. What a gem she had been during the past weeks, quietly arranging things so that all their family and friends needs were attended. Elizabeth need not worry. The world outside the walls of their cabin seemed solemnly quiet. Donning one of the warm robes her husband had seen fit to have awaiting them in their little refuge, Elizabeth got out of bed and crept across the room to peer out the window. She opened the curtains and wiped a bit frost from the windowpane. Joy akin to her days as a child washed over her. "It is snowing again!" She tore her eyes away from the picturesque snow covered landscape. "Come and have a look."

She regarded his handsome person and noble mien and began to consider that the prospect of his surrendering their cosy bed as she had just done was the furthest thing from his mind. Raising one hand to the back of his head, he rested against his satiny pillow.

"There is no surprise there. This is Derbyshire. Pray come back to bed. I find I am missing you already and that will not do, especially in view of how long I planned this little escape for the two of us."

Deciding to acquiesce, she drew the curtains

closed and surrendered her spot at the window. Her mind wandered to her family and friends, whose travels may have yet to see them safely in their homes. If only everyone could be as fortunate as were the two of them at that moment. "I pray all is well with our family and friends and that they all arrive safely at their destinations."

"I share your sentiments. We must trust that all is well in that regard."

Now back by his side, where she once again felt warm and cherished, Elizabeth nestled close to Darcy. She took his hand in hers, raised it to her lips, and brushed a kiss across his knuckles.

He brushed his thumb across her lips. "It looks like you got your Christmas wish after all, my love."

She half smiled. "As much as I enjoy the fact that Lord Holland and Lucy have found each other and they are to be man and wife, there is one wish that would have pleased me more."

"Pray tell."

"That you and I were to be blessed with child."

"There is always next Christmas."

"Indeed. A great deal can happen between now and then."

"Quite true, my dearest, loveliest Elizabeth,"

whispered Darcy. Moistening their lips and closing their eyes, Darcy and Elizabeth drew nearer to each other.

What started as a sweet kiss slowly gave way to a stirring surge of passion. Amidst the pleasing sounds of the roaring fireplace and two young lovers violently in love, one thing was certain—Mr. and Mrs. Darcy would indeed while away the rest of that wondrous wintry day in bed.

The Author

P. O. Dixon is a writer as well as an entertainer. Historical England and its days of yore fascinate her. She, in particular, loves the Regency period with its strict mores and oh so proper decorum. Her ardent appreciation of Jane Austen's timeless works set her on the writer's journey. Visit podixon.com and find out more about Dixon's writings.

Author's Other Books

§ **Pride and Prejudice Untold Series:**

To Have His Cake (and Eat It Too): Mr. Darcy's Tale (Book 1)
What He Would Not Do: Mr. Darcy's Tale Continues (Book 2)
Lady Harriette: Fitzwilliam's Heart and Soul (Book 3)

§ **Darcy and the Young Knight's Quest Series:**

He Taught Me to Hope (Book 1)
The Mission: He Taught Me to Hope Christmas Vignette (Book 2)
Hope and Sensibility (Book 3)

Other Pride and Prejudice "What-if" Stories:

A Lasting Love Affair: Darcy and Elizabeth
Still a Young Man: Darcy Is In Love
Bewitched, Body and Soul: Miss Elizabeth Bennet
Matter of Trust: The Shades of Pemberley
Love Will Grow: A Pride and Prejudice Story
Only a Heartbeat Away: Pride and Prejudice Novella
Almost Persuaded: Miss Mary King
Pride and Sensuality: A Darcy and Elizabeth Short Story
Expecting His Proposal: A Darcy and Elizabeth Short Story
A Tender Moment: A Darcy and Elizabeth Short Story

21691411R00086

Printed in Great Britain
by Amazon